A MURDEROUS MARRIAGE

THE ADMIRAL SHACKLEFORD MYSTERIES
BOOK TWO

BEVERLEY WATTS

Copyright © 2017 BaR Publishing
All rights reserved. No part of this publication may be reproduced, stored or transmitted in any form or by any means, electronic, mechanical, photocopying, recording, scanning or otherwise without written permission from the publisher.

It is illegal to copy this book, post it to a website, or distribute it by any other means without permission.

This novel is entirely a work of fiction. The names, characters and incidents portrayed in it are the work of the author's imagination. Any resemblance to actual persons, living or dead, events or localities is entirely coincidental.

BaR Publishing has no responsibility for the persistence or accuracy of URL's for external or third party Internet Websites referred to in this publication and does not guarantee that any content on such Websites is, or will remain, accurate or appropriate.

Designations used by companies to distinguish their products are often claimed as trademarks. All brand names and product names used in this book and on its cover are trade names, service marks, trademarks and registered trademarks of their respective owners. The publishers and the book are not associated with any product or vendor mentioned in this book. None of the companies referenced within the book have endorsed the book.

Cover Design by Covers by Karen

CHAPTER 1

'These bollocking sandwiches have been dead nearly as long as old Barney,' the Admiral complained in a voice loud enough to be heard two funerals over.

'Shush dad,' Tory muttered in a heated whisper. 'We're not here so you can help yourself to a free lunch.'

The Admiral regarded his daughter dubiously. 'Why else do you think people come to funerals Victory? Just take a look at all these so called oppos and tell me they aren't here for the scran.'

Tory closed her eyes and counted to ten. They'd been at the Wake ten minutes and already she was regretting her decision to accompany her father to the funeral of his old friend Barney Bennett. Of course, she used the word *friend* in the loosest sense of the word. To her knowledge Admiral Charles Shackleford RN (retired) had only managed to hang on to two close friends in his entire life, and both of them were mostly too scared to tell him to go and sling his hook.

Sighing she looked around to see if she recognized anyone. The Admiral and Barney Bennett had known each other since her father first came to Dartmouth as the Commodore of Britannia Royal Naval

College. A lowly lieutenant at the time, Barney had been her father's secretary and general dog's body.

The naval college was the Royal Navy's premier officer training establishment, towering over the small town of Dartmouth at the mouth of the beautiful River Dart since the early nineteen hundreds.

Although the Admiral had only remained in post there for a little over two years, he apparently considered the running of it his finest hour, (even though it's generally well known that his superiors were more interested in keeping him out of trouble). Tory was fairly sure that her father still privately considered himself in charge, and as his home (quaintly called The Admiralty) overlooked the College's hallowed halls on the other side of the river, he was in a prime position to ensure that standards remained ship shape and Bristol fashion.

So, the Wake was being held in the Wardroom of the College in honour of Barney's time there.

Tory knew most of the people present by sight. She'd lived in Dartmouth her whole life, and even now, married to arguably the world's most famous movie star, she couldn't think of anywhere she'd rather live, even if it was sometimes a bit too close to her unpredictable, irresponsible, not to mention completely self-centred father.

She turned back to the Admiral, just in time to see him heading determinedly over to Barney's widow. 'Damn,' she muttered, swiftly knocking back her sherry. There was no way she could leave her old man to hand out his brand of condolences to the late Barney Bennett's grieving spouse.

Hurrying after her father, she wondered, not for the first time, whether Mabel's sudden attack of the flu might have been a deliberate ploy. The Admiral was a ticking time bomb at the best of times, but in a sensitive gathering such as this one, he was a disaster waiting to happen.

Breathless, she came up behind her father just in time to hear him say, 'So, old Barney was your third husband was he? How did the other two pop their clogs then…?'

∞∞∞

'I'm telling you right now Jimmy lad, there's some kind of skullduggery going on. Old Barney was the third bollocking husband to die on her.'

'Some would just call that unfortunate Sir,' his old friend Jimmy offered mildly. 'Anyway, I thought Barney was killed in a car accident.'

'His brakes failed Jimmy. Don't you think that's damn dodgy?' the Admiral responded, waving at the barmaid to bring them both another pint.

The two men were sitting on their customary stools at the bar in their local watering hole. The Ship Inn was mostly frequented by regulars and served good honest home cooking – the sort that put a spring in your step and a lining round your middle. None of that bloody bunny grub as the Admiral referred to the current penchant for so called gastropub fare - and of course their pickled eggs were legendary.

It was nicely cozy, and despite it being the middle of May, there was a roaring fire in the grate which the Admiral's old Springer spaniel Pickles was happily snoring in front of.

'The police didn't seem to think so Sir,' Jimmy answered after taking a sip of his pint. 'I read in the paper that the verdict was accidental death.'

'Accidental my arse,' the Admiral muttered. 'I'm taking Mabel to pay our respects to Barney's mother this afternoon. Thought it was a bit bloody telling that she wasn't at the funeral.'

Jimmy sighed. Ever since the two of them had solved the murder at

The Two Bridges hotel, the Admiral had taken to seeing jiggery-pokery in everything.

'I thought she had the flu, you know the same virus that had Mabel laid up.'

The Admiral shook his head and murmured darkly, 'You mark my words Jimmy, there's something fishy going on.'

'What did her other husbands die of?' Jimmy asked suddenly, interested in spite of himself.

'Victory dragged me away before I could find out, but Birdie – I ask you what kind of a name is that? I've never seen anyone less bird like. Her thighs were right knacker crackers.

'Anyway, where was I? Oh yes, *Birdie* was hiding something I could tell. She was too bloody upset.'

Jimmy stared at the Admiral in bewilderment. 'She was at her husband's funeral Sir. She was bound to be upset. Please tell me you didn't say anything to distress her further.'

'Didn't get the chance. She was blubbing into the arms of some woman who claimed to be her daughter. Whoever she was, she certainly didn't issue from old Barney's loins. I don't want to speak ill of the dead, but you must admit he had a face like a bulldog chewing a wasp.'

'So what happened Sir?' Jimmy interrupted hastily, feeling sorry for Tory who'd no doubt drawn the short straw when it came to accompanying the Admiral to Barney Bennett's Wake in the absence of his partner Mabel.

'Well, the so-called daughter was doing a good job of dealing with Birdie's sniveling. Victory said how sorry she was and all that malarkey, then she made our excuses, and we left. I didn't even get any bloody cake.'

Miriam Bennett lived in a large house on one of Dartmouth's many narrow lanes that wound higgledy piggledy away from the river and up the hill. Driving up them was a challenge, and many a skilled motorist had ended up hanging over the edge of a forty foot drop looking down at a cottage garden more suitable to a mountain goat.

On this occasion, Mabel's ear-splitting scream was the only reason they didn't end up causing a swathe of devastation right down to the harbour below, much in the manner of snakes and ladders.

Screeching to a halt with a muttered oath, the Admiral regretfully decided that all thoughts of murder and mayhem would need to be temporarily parked if they were to arrive at their destination in one piece.

Five minutes later, they were knocking on Miriam Bennett's door - pale, sweating, but fortunately intact.

'Oh my goodness, what on earth happened to you?' Miriam asked in alarm as she opened the door to their ashen faces.

Ushering them in, she sat them both down in the sitting room and hurried off to make tea.

While Mabel fussed around in her bag for a bottle of smelling salts, the Admiral allowed his mind to return to the distinctly shady demise of Barney Bennett – although he had to admit, if the accident had happened coming to or from his mother's house, not only was it understandable, it was a wonder he didn't take anyone else with him.

Glancing about, he got to his feet and wandered over to the large ornate fireplace, groaning under the weight of family photographs. Studying each one in turn, he wasn't surprised to note that there were none of old Barney's widow. He nodded his head thoughtfully. Definitely no love lost there.

Placing the last photo back, he made his way over to the baby grand piano in the corner of the room. The dust proclaimed it hadn't been played for quite a while and seemed to be merely another flat surface for more family pictures.

As the Admiral stared at the younger features of Barney, he tried to recall what had happened to his first wife. He picked up the photo of a slim laughing woman. Her name had been Linda he remembered and she'd died of cancer, years ago now. There'd been no children. He wondered what Barney's relationship with Birdie's daughter had been like.

Hearing a noise behind him, he turned round in time to see Miriam bringing in tea and biscuits. Setting the tray down on the table, she fussed around Mabel who was leaning faintly against the back of the chair waving smelling salts back and forth under her nose.

'I keep telling the council they've got to do something about this road,' Miriam complained, pouring the first cup and handing it to Mabel.

'Like what?' asked the Admiral bluntly, coming to sit down. 'Short of knocking down every bloody house between here and the ferry, there's really not a lot they can do except ban cars altogether.' He held out his hand to take a cup of tea from Miriam. 'Did Barney's accident happen on this road?'

Mabel glared over at him and leaned forward to take the small woman's hand. 'We were so sorry to hear about it,' she murmured a little awkwardly. 'Barney was such a nice, kind man. It must be devastating for all of you.'

Miriam sniffed and fumbled for her handkerchief, nodding. 'It was a total shock,' she answered, dabbing her eyes. 'Barney had been so happy lately, what with Birdie and Angela coming into his life.'

'Angela's Birdie's daughter?' the Admiral interrupted brusquely. Miriam nodded. 'She's a lovely girl. Always so pleasant, and of course she's devoted to her mother.'

'Do you get on with your daughter in law?' asked the Admiral directly, helping himself to a custard cream.

'I... I... we don't see each other often... I mean we didn't, when Barney was alive. It... well, it wasn't the same, you know,' floundered Miriam. 'Birdie was quite a bit younger than Barney. When he and Linda were married, they used to come up here all the time, but I don't think Birdie has much use for mollycoddling old ladies.'

'Oh I'm sure you'll be a great comfort to one another dear,' Mabel disagreed. 'You've both lost someone you loved greatly. It will bring you closer, I can feel it.' She patted Miriam's hand before leaning back and taking a ginger nut.

They sat for the next few minutes in silence, only punctuated by the Admiral dipping his custard cream into his tea. Just as the quiet started to become oppressive and Charles Shackleford was wondering if he could get away with asking Miriam if she thought her son had been bumped off, the small woman sighed and placed her cup and saucer onto the tray.

'You know it's funny really,' she murmured sadly. 'Birdie should have been in the car too. They were going over to Exeter to visit friends, but Birdie cried off at the last minute, said she had a migraine.

'Strange isn't it,' she added softly, 'how something as simple as a headache can change the whole course of your life. If my daughter in law hadn't taken to her bed that night, she'd probably be dead now too.'

CHAPTER 2

'You've really got to try and be a bit more circumspect Charlie.' The Admiral couldn't help but wince at Mabel's frosty tone. 'The poor woman has just lost her son and you're talking about whether she gets on with her daughter in law.'

'I don't care what you say Mabel,' he stated belligerently as he drove the car onto the Upper Car Ferry to take them back across the River Dart towards the Admiralty, 'There's something not right about the whole thing.'

'Well the accident didn't happen near Miriam's house,' Mabel retorted, choosing for a moment to ignore the Admiral's less than respectful response. 'It would have been a disaster if Barney's brakes had failed on that hill.'

The Admiral glanced over at her pensively. 'I should think the whole bollocking load of horlicks was pretty disastrous in old Barney eyes, but you might have a point there old girl.

'I wonder if Barney and Birdie were supposed to have called on Miriam before they headed off to Exeter. If someone had tampered with the brakes, it would be a sure fire bet they'd come down that hill a lot bloody quicker than they went up it.'

'Well I might see Miriam at the Ladies Afloat meeting on Friday,' Mabel responded before continuing tartly, 'I'll see if I can ask the question without employing your bull in a china shop tactics Charlie.'

The Admiral flinched again. He had to admit, if only privately, that sometimes living with Mabel was no better than living with his daughter. He sighed. He'd swapped one bloody nag for another.

They were silent as he negotiated the car off the ferry on the opposite side of the river. But as they began to wind up the hill towards the Admiralty, Charles Shackleford thought he'd better employ some damage limitation if he wanted any of Mabel's homemade steak and kidney pie he knew was waiting to go in the oven.

'You're very astute my dove, I really don't know what I'd do without you,' he murmured patting Mabel's knee.

Mabel gave a muttered, 'Humph,' as they drove through the Admiralty gates. 'You'd be a damn sight thinner Charlie, that's for sure…'

∞∞∞

'So where did this so-called accident happen then?' The Admiral was practically sitting in Jimmy's lap as the small man brought up details of Barney Bennett's crash on the internet.

'It says here his brakes failed as he was driving down the slip road onto the A38.'

'Didn't the plod think it was a bit strange that his damn brakes failed all of a sudden?'

Jimmy shook his head. 'It just says they're not treating the accident as suspicious.'

They were sitting in the Admiral's study while Mabel rustled up some tea and stickies with the moral support of Jimmy's wife Emily.

It was Saturday morning and the Admiral had called an emergency meeting after Mabel had discovered through sensitive probing (her words) that Barney and Birdie were indeed supposed to have popped in to see Miriam before setting off for Exeter. Apparently Birdie's sudden migraine attack prevented the flying visit...

By the time Barney had tucked his beloved up in bed, drawn the curtains and called his stepdaughter, there hadn't been enough time to call on his mother if he was to arrive punctually at their friends' house.

'The thing is Jimmy,' the Admiral continued, 'In this day an...' He was interrupted as the study door crashed open and Mabel tottered in carrying a tray nearly as big as she was. Beside her, Pickles charged in, tail wagging excitedly, having clearly spotted the coffee and walnut cake sliding ominously to the front of the tray. Only Jimmy's quick thinking prevented all the spaniel's prayers of the last ten years being answered at once. The small man managed to grab hold of the tray and place it on the desk, just as Emily entered behind Mabel carrying a large plate of homemade shortbread.

Any rebuke the Admiral was about to utter died at the sight of the still warm shortbread, and standing up, he gallantly offered one of the ladies his seat, and helped himself to a biscuit while he was at it.

'The thing is,' he stated self-importantly after the tea had been poured and the cake shared out. He paused for effect and took a large bite of his shortbread, leaning back against the edge of the desk in what he imagined was a sophisticated pose. Unfortunately, the effect was slightly spoiled as his second effort came out as, 'Fefinghis,' while he liberally sprayed the other three with chewed up bits of biscuit. The only one remotely impressed was Pickles.

'For God's sake sit down and get on with it Charlie,' Emily muttered, brushing the crushed up bits off her skirt directly into the mouth of the eager spaniel.

The Admiral scowled at Jimmy's wife for effectively stealing his thunder, but nevertheless, quickly swallowed the rest of his shortbread and sat down at his desk.

However, not one to allow the small embarrassment of gobbed up biscuit to dampen his flair for the dramatic, the Admiral steepled his fingers in his best Sherlock Holmes manner, and leaning forward towards the other three, pronounced melodramatically, 'Ladies and Gentlemen, we have another case. Operation *Murderous Marriages* is on...'

The rest of the morning was spent trawling the internet trying to find out the unfortunate ends of Birdie Barnett's two former husbands.

The Admiral and Jimmy used Tory's old computer, while Emily and Mabel once again made use of Emily's iPad. Three quarters of the coffee cake and fifteen pieces of shortbread later, Jimmy finally came up with a reference to Birdie's first husband, and it was every bit as mysterious as the Admiral had hoped.

'Apparently he was a keen sailor.' Jimmy quickly scanned the article he'd found, then read out loud, 'Marcus Tennant, aged forty-six, was reported as having fallen overboard whilst racing his yacht, Tempest, in the Cowes Regatta. His body was never recovered, and after a futile search lasting nearly two months, he was reluctantly declared to have drowned. He leaves a wife and teenage daughter.

'In an interview, his widow Birdie Tennant described her husband as a caring and thoughtful individual, loved by all who knew him. She then went on to say that she and her daughter Angela would miss him more than they could say.'

Jimmy turned the computer screen round so they could all see the pictures. In the first one, a smiling, much slimmer Birdie stared out at them, her arms draped around a distinguished looking man wearing a pair of sunglasses.

'I know Birdie was a lot younger than Barney, but looking at that photo, I think she was a lot younger than her first husband too,' mused Emily.

Mabel pointed at the second picture of a teenage Angela snuggling up to her father. 'The poor mite must have adored him,' the matron murmured sadly, shaking her head, 'It's a good job she had her mother to lean on, or who knows what might have happened to her.'

The third picture was of a yacht. In the foreground a laughing Marcus Tennant had the helm while two other muscle types pulled hard at the winches.

With a sigh, the Admiral leaned back and helped himself to the last piece of shortbread. 'So that's husband number one,' he reflected, waiting until he'd finished chewing this time before speculating. 'All we know is that he supposedly fell overboard, even though he was apparently a very experienced sailor, and I have to say, looking at those photos, pretty damn fit. Doesn't add up, does it?'

'We can't rule out an accident yet Sir,' Jimmy offered, pulling the monitor round to face him again, 'Even the most experienced sportsmen make mistakes.'

Going back to Google, he tapped on *Images* at the top of the page. 'We need to find out what happened to her second husband, and exactly how long she waited after Marcus's death before she went ahead and tied the knot.'

It was late afternoon before they gave up and called it a day. There didn't seem to be any reference anywhere to Birdie's second husband.

'There's got to be some mention of the bloody man somewhere,' the Admiral grumbled, 'He can't just have disappeared into thin air.'

'What about a death certificate?' Mabel asked suddenly.

A MURDEROUS MARRIAGE

'Without a bollocking name, we don't know where to look,' the Admiral responded tetchily.

'Could we find out what name Birdie went by when she married Barney?' Emily asked eagerly, 'She might have used her second husband's surname.'

'It's possible I suppose, if we can find out where they were married. Did they get hitched here in Dartmouth? I can't remember being asked to the wedding.' The Admiral's retort was indignant as if he couldn't imagine anyone not wanting him attending their nuptials.

'No, I think it was somewhere quite exotic,' Emily murmured thoughtfully. 'I'm almost certain they had one of these beach weddings and came back with it all done and dusted.'

'A fat accomplice,' added Mabel knowingly.

Jimmy had been silent throughout the whole exchange, so his eventual heartfelt sigh drew all their attention. All three stared at him expectantly.

'I hate to say this Sir,' the small man said at length, 'But I think the only way we're going to find out anything at all about Birdie Bennett's second husband is to ask her...'

In the event, they didn't have the opportunity to come up with a cunning plan to interview Birdie Bennett until a couple of days later.

To the Admiral's horror, Mabel had arranged a day trip to the zoo. That would have been bad enough, but the idea was that they took the carpet crawler along. Charles Shackleford couldn't believe it. In his book Sunday was reserved for two pints at The Ship, a slap up roast followed by a couple of glasses of Port and forty winks in front of the box.

'What the bollocking hell were you thinking Mabel?' he asked outraged, when he could finally bring himself to speak, 'This is a bloody impingement on my liberty. I've a good mind to damn well send you over the wall.'

'First of all Charlie, you don't have the authority to send me to the toilet, let alone a military jail, and secondly, I thought it was high time you got to know your grandson.' Mabel's voice had a horrible finality about it and even though the Admiral opened his mouth to reply, nothing actually came out of it.

'What about Victory and Noah?' he shouted desperately up the stairs half an hour later, 'There's no way they'd allow us to take their first born out for the whole day.'

'Well that's where you're wrong Charlie,' Mabel responded calmly as she came down dressed in *jeans* of all things. The Admiral felt as though he'd fallen down a rabbit hole.

'Tory and Noah were delighted when I asked them. Of course your daughter was a bit anxious that you might not be quite as keen, but I assured her that the whole thing was your idea and you can't wait to spend some quality time with your first grandchild…'

CHAPTER 3

Charles Shackleford couldn't remember the last time he was so knackered. No, scratch that, he could. It was when he'd hiked through the Borneo jungle as a Midshipman to be a spotter for some Naval gunfire support fifty years ago.

When they'd picked Isaac up earlier, Victory had given him a three page list of dos and don'ts, together with a bag containing everything they needed to survive should World War Three happen to break out before they got home.

They walked the length and breadth of Paignton Zoo. They saw lions, tigers, monkeys, rhinos, kangaroos, zebras, giraffes, crocodiles, snakes and flamingos... and Isaac slept through the whole thing.

Of course he woke up just as they were about to tuck in to a nice plate of fish and chips in the park's café.

The Admiral was sent off to commandeer a high chair. Easier said than done. The café had more ankle biters in it than a bloody nursery. The only high chair he could find was covered in left over baked beans and something resembling super glue which he only discovered as he carried it over to their table.

'He can't sit in that,' tssked Mabel. 'Look in the bag for the nappy wipes.'

The Admiral opened the bag and poked his head helplessly inside. 'Like looking for a bloody needle in a haystack,' he muttered rummaging around half heartedly. Ten minutes later, he still hadn't found the wipes.

'For God's sake Charlie, you couldn't find your way out of a wet paper bag,' Mabel said crossly. 'Here, you take the baby, while I look for the wipes.'

Of course, as soon as she plonked Isaac into his grandfather's arms, the baby started crying, or more accurately screaming. While Mabel located the wipes and hurriedly cleaned up the highchair, the Admiral jogged his grandson up and down watching in distaste as snot and dribble slowly made its way down Isaac's face and onto his shoulder. 'There, there,' Charles Shackleford muttered trying to hold the squirming bundle away from his nice clean sweater.

'Right then, you can put him in Charlie.'

Sighing with relief, the Admiral held Isaac over the highchair, finally managing to stuff him into the seat by using a similar tactic he employed to force the last pair of socks into his sock drawer. Not surprisingly little Isaac upped the game.

'WHAT'S WRONG WITH HIM?' shouted the Admiral over the din.

'YOU'VE UPSET HIM,' yelled back Mabel, 'AND I THINK HE'S HUNGRY.' She started rummaging around in the bag again, searching for the tuna sandwiches Tory had packed.

'I'LL GIVE HIM A CHIP,' the Admiral bellowed, just as Mabel shouted, 'WHY DON'T YOU GIVE HIM A CHIP?'

And just like that the bawling stopped.

The rug rat then proceeded to eat three quarters of the Admiral's chips while using the tasty piece of cod as a dartboard for the set of car keys he flatly refused to give up. The resulting mess resembled something out of *Alien*.

And now to add insult to injury, here he was actually *about to change a nappy*. The Admiral couldn't believe the obnoxious smell that was drifting up from Isaac's nether regions as he carried the wriggling bundle towards the baby changing facilities. Mabel was marching determinedly in front of him and the Admiral knew she'd only made him carry his grandson to foil any possibility of him making a run for it before things got messy.

'Right,' Mabel said in a matter of fact voice when they got into the baby changing room. 'Lie him down on the mat Charlie and go round to his top half.'

They quickly realized that even though Isaac wasn't quite yet one, he had the strength of a twenty year old when it came to having his bottom changed. Mabel hurriedly took out the clean nappy and a large wad of wipes which she placed in a strategic position next to the Admiral's left hand. 'You ready Charlie?' she asked crisply when they were in position.

The Admiral nodded tensely while trying to distract his grandson from the upcoming operation by performing an admittedly substandard version of *Round and Round the Garden*. Or at least that was his intention, but Isaac had obviously been used to the real McCoy and the hands the Admiral had been holding quickly found their way to the disaster area that was the other end.

'CHARLIE,' Mabel screeched as Isaac managed to grab hold of the dirty nappy in his fist.

'SHIT, SHIT, SHIT,' yelled the Admiral rather appropriately as he made futile attempts to grab hold of his grandson's flailing fingers. At the same time, Mabel tugged at the soiled pad under Isaac's bottom, which finally jerked free with such force, it sailed through the air before landing face down on the Admiral's shoe.

By the time they'd got themselves and Isaac cleaned up, there was a huge queue of disgruntled parents and babies, all waiting outside to use the facilities. As they came out, a couple of the more belligerent parents started talking loudly about people having no consideration for others. The Admiral, who was carrying Isaac, simply stopped and gave them The Look which he usually reserved for subordinates who'd overstepped the mark. Gradually the muttering stopped, and the Admiral leaned down to his freshly washed grandson who was busy poking the car keys into his grandfather's ear, and whispered, 'That's how it's done Isaac lad, that's how it's done.'

It was now nearly half past three and the Admiral knew Victory would be getting a bit skittish, wondering where they were. Strangely though, he no longer felt the urge to rush off back to Dartmouth as quickly as possible and suggested to Mabel they have a quick shufti at the gorilla enclosure so at least Isaac wouldn't have missed everything. Mabel simply nodded and smiled to herself as she watched the large man march up the hill with his grandson singing, *'Oh the grand old Duke of York.'*

All in all, a satisfactory day...

It was almost five pm by the time they arrived back at Noah and Victory's house set high on the headland overlooking the mouth of the Dart. Isaac had slept most of the way again, but woke up when the Admiral lifted him from the car. Luckily he didn't start yelling this time and the Admiral was curiously reluctant to hand him over to Tory who it had to be said did seem a bit on the anxious side, although she did her best to hide it. Tory's little dog Dotty barked excitedly, dancing around their ankles until the Admiral gave in and bent to give her a fuss.

'Do you have time to stop for a bite to eat?' asked Noah coming up beside his wife and taking their son out of her arms.

The Admiral glanced over at Mabel. He had no idea what she'd planned for dinner. 'That would be lovely,' she said firmly, giving him the distinct feeling that he could well have been heading home for toast and marmite. Charles Shackleford nodded his head enthusiastically, thinking of the more than adequate bottle of Port he knew Noah had stashed away in his cellar.

The Admiral patted his stomach contentedly and sipped his second glass of Port. All was definitely well with the world. Little Isaac had been put to bed, they'd just finished a first rate cottage pie and Mabel had agreed to drive home.

'So when are you going to start filming your next film Noah?' Mabel asked, obviously hoping to get the jump on her cronies at the Women's Institute.

Noah smiled ruefully. 'You're not the first one to ask me that Mabel. Over the last few weeks, the number of paparazzi hiding in the bushes outside has increased at the same rate as the rumours I'm about to announce my next project.' He sighed, taking hold of Tory's hand. 'It's been amazing having these few months at home with my family, but I guess it's time to get back in the saddle.' He grinned, all seriousness gone. 'And that's exactly what I'm about to do. It's a Western. Filming starts in July.'

Tory batted his shoulder, using his hand as leverage. 'He can't wait. The last few weeks he's been swaggering around and drawling like *John Wayne*. I'll be glad to get rid of him.' They both laughed.

'Will you be away for long?' asked the Admiral in alarm, thinking of babysitting duties. While he could honestly say hand on heart that he'd enjoyed their day out, he was convinced he'd be pushing up daisies with old Barney if he had to do it too often.

'He'll be filming in southern Spain for the first few months,' said Tory, excitement colouring her voice, 'We're looking for a large villa to rent so Isaac and I can go out to join him.' The Admiral nodded, relief swamping him, until Tory's next words.

'We were hoping that you and Mabel would come out to join us dad. I've already mentioned it to Kit and thankfully Jason will be on terminal leave with the RN by then, so they're both definitely up for it.' She paused laughing before continuing, 'And of course Freddy said he'd camp outside on our back door step if we didn't invite him.'

The Admiral shuddered at the idea of sharing a villa with Tory's best friends and he was about to say so, when Mabel got in first. 'That would be absolutely fabulous. A chance to spend more time with little Isaac. You could take him swimming Charlie – you'd love that wouldn't you?' The Admiral looked over at her in horror. The last time he'd worn a pair of swimming trunks was in the sixties.

'I... err... well... what will you do with Dotty?' He pounced on the lifeline with all the enthusiasm of a drowning man.

'She'll be coming with us of course,' smiled Tory, stroking the little dog who was contentedly snoring on the sofa having consumed her own dinner as well as all of Isaac's leftovers.

'And Pickles can stay with my son Oscar,' Mabel decided with a terrible finality. The Admiral stared in dismay between his daughter and Mabel, completely out of ideas. He must have looked like a rabbit trapped in a set of headlights because Tory said softly, 'I'd really like it if you'd come dad, if only for a few days. Please say you'll think about it.'

Which of course sealed his fate.

Noah, trying hard not to laugh, decided that a change of subject was in order. 'So what have you been up to Charlie since you became Dartmouth's answer to Sherlock Holmes?' he asked, genuinely interested.

Modestly waving away the actor's reference to his local celebrity status, Charles Shackleford nevertheless visibly brightened up, and leaning forward, he enthusiastically began to recount the details of their latest case....

'And now we need to find out about her second husband,' he finished, oblivious to his daughter's horrified face, 'So we're going to trump up some excuse to go and have a chat.'

'Not you surely dad?' Tory asked, not bothering to keep the alarm out of her voice. 'There's no way Mrs. Bennett will talk to you after your insensitivity at her husband's funeral.

'And anyway,' she continued, desperately now, 'There's no evidence of foul play is there?'

The Admiral sighed. He loved his daughter but sometimes wondered how she'd ever managed to bag a looker like Noah. Patiently he explained, using the same tone he'd used to Isaac earlier. 'That's why we need to speak to Birdie Bennett.'

Tory groaned and put her head into her hands, ignoring her husband's silent shaking laughter beside her. 'Dad, you could end up getting arrested for harassment if you pursue this. And you might remember that it's not that long ago you actually got out of bloody prison.' She was referring to a whole load of shenanigans her father had been involved in the year before.

To her surprise Mabel chose that moment to chip in. 'Don't you worry Tory, I won't let your father get himself into trouble. Emily and I have decided that we'll be the ones going to have a chat with Birdie – woman to woman. Charlie will brief us before we go in. We'll be just like Elmo and Louis.'

Mabel could see that for some reason her words didn't appear to make Tory feel any better. The Admiral's daughter blinked and simply looked confused.

'I think you mean Thelma and Louise,' Noah offered, still trying to keep a straight face, 'But you might want to think of another duo Mabel. To my knowledge the two ladies weren't detectives and actually drove off a cliff at the end of that movie.'

The Admiral frowned and Mabel looked shocked. 'We won't have to do that after we've spoken to Birdie will we Charlie?'

The Admiral sighed. This was what happened when you didn't have the right raw material to work with. While it was true that sending in Mabel and Emily would probably get them more Intel from the widow, how on earth was he going to make sure they stuck to their scripts?

'If one of you has a tablet, you could use one of those walkie-talkie apps,' Noah suggested, just as the Admiral was about to throw his hands in the air and announce he would be conducting the interview himself, even though he'd no doubt be as welcome as a fart in a space suit.

'What do they do?' Charles Shackleford asked sensing possible salvation.

'Well,' the actor continued, ignoring his wife's glare from beside him. 'You can send Mabel and Emily in, both wearing a wire in their ear, while you sit in a car or something outside and give them instructions through your mouthpiece.'

The Admiral stared at Noah, totally speechless for a second. Then he leaned forward with a broad grin which completely put the fear of God into his daughter. 'That's a bloody cracker of an idea Noah, and I think it definitely deserves another glass of Port to celebrate...'

∞∞∞∞

'I really can't believe you Noah Westbrook. You of all people know exactly what my father's capable of.

'In what universe could it possibly be a good idea to give my father - who let's be honest gives a whole new meaning to unpredictable and eccentric - a veritable smoking gun and tell him to go off and play with it.' Tory wasted no time in rounding on her unrepentant husband as soon as her father and Mabel had left.

Noah opened his mouth to make a lighthearted quip, then saw his wife was genuinely upset. Sighing, he shook his head and took her resistant body into his arms. 'Honey, I'm sorry. Sometimes I just can't help it with your old man. He's the most entertaining guy I've ever come across in the whole of my acting career.'

'Well I'm so pleased you're entertained.' Tory's voice was muffled against his chest, but he could tell she wasn't mollified in the least. Leaning back he tipped her chin up to look at him.

'I think you're doing him a disservice Tory. I know he's unpredictable, and eccentric, and selfish, and slippery, and evasive…, and all of those things. But maybe he's not as foolish as you think. He and Jimmy actually solved that murder in The Two Bridges hotel. You never know, his instincts might be spot on with this one.'

'The only time my father's instincts are spot on is when he's trying to get himself out of the hole he's jumped into,' Tory answered in a slightly calmer voice, pulling away. 'Trouble follows him around like a bad smell, you know it does, and you've just handed him a bloody great cow pat.' She shook her head and headed to the bathroom.

'I really am sorry honey,' Noah apologized again, wandering in after her, 'But, look at it this way. At least if he's not in the same room as Birdie Bennett, he's less likely to get arrested…'

CHAPTER 4

'Right then, according to my sources, Birdie Bennett is the owner of something called Birdie's Groom Room on Victoria Street.'

'We knew that Charlie, it's a beauty salon. Agnes Dewbury says it's a bit pricey but it's very good.'

The Admiral stared at Mabel in disbelief. 'How long have you been aware of this?' he asked in a strangled voice. The elderly matron frowned.

'Well, I'm not sure. I remember when Birdie first arrived in Dartmouth – about five years ago I think it was.' Emily nodded in agreement. 'She bought that scruffy old hairdressers - what was it called Emily?'

'Tresses Bien,' supplied her friend helpfully.

'That's right, horrible place it was,' Mabel continued with a shudder. 'They turned Lydia Johnson Wood's hair bright green. I think she said she was going to sue them so the owners did a runner in the middle of the night.

'Birdie gave the place a revamp and opened up about six months later.'

Jimmy and the Admiral looked at each other. 'So why did you just let me and Jimmy sit here for the last three hours trying to find out what the bloody woman did for a living?' demanded the Admiral trying hard to keep his temper.

'You didn't ask dear. We thought you were enjoying yourselves. Are you both ready for a cuppa?'

∞∞∞

'So what did you say you were booked in for Emily?'

'I'm going to have my legs waxed,' answered Emily self importantly. 'I was going to leave it at that, but Jim suggested I get my top lip done while I'm at it. He's so generous sometimes.'

Mabel nodded in agreement and looked down at her brochure. 'Charlie said it's important that we each have something done at the same time. So if you're waxing...' she pursed her lips and glanced down the columns, 'Maybe I can have my eyelashes and eyebrows dyed.'

'Ooh I don't know dear,' responded Emily doubtfully, 'What happens if she spots the microphone in your ear? Why don't you go for a nice pedicure?' She looked down at Mabel's feet and refrained from pointing out that they actually looked a bit like a hobbit's. 'Your feet could definitely do with a little bit of love and attention,' she said delicately instead.

Mabel frowned a little mutinously - she'd fancied the idea of having her eyebrows done like *Joan Crawford*. 'You could have your toenails done in that colour you liked on Agnes,' Emily added slyly, seeing her friend's indecision.

'Hot Culture,' Mabel agreed brightening. 'What time shall we book for?'

'We'll have to take whatever time we can get in together,' responded Emily matter of factly, 'But we'll try for later on in the afternoon. That way, Charlie will find it easier to park close enough to get a reception on my Pad thingy. We'll go and book it when we've done here.'

It was Thursday afternoon and they were sitting in the Royal Castle Hotel waiting for Tory and her friend Freddy to join them while Noah took Isaac to the park. Tory's best friend Kit Davies had just got engaged to the dashing, though somewhat dour, Captain Jason Buchannan, and their friends were organizing a surprise party for both of them. Tory intended to hold it at her and Noah's house, bringing in outside caterers to take care of the difficult bits.

Mabel and Emily were there so that Tory could make sure they had nothing disastrous planned in relation to the late Barney Bennett's widow. Of course they didn't know that. Both matrons thought they were helping with the vol-au-vents…

'Hello ladies, if I didn't bat for the other side, I swear I would be swooning with lust right now.'

Freddy's dulcet tones rang out from the doorway, causing both Mabel and Emily to giggle in delight. He posed in affectation for a few seconds, making sure that everyone caught his good side, before being shoved unceremoniously into the room by Tory who'd come up behind him. 'Move over *Errol Flynn* I've got precisely thirty minutes to get this show on the road before Isaac starts yelling for his tea.'

'Time enough for a spot of fizz then,' Freddy murmured heading determinedly over to the bar.

'God, yes please,' Tory mumbled to his back before sitting down at their table. 'How are you ladies?' she asked with a warm, though slightly nervous smile, 'Done any interviewing lately?'

∞∞∞∞∞

'We've booked the treatments for Monday morning first thing,' Emily announced over a glass of sherry at the Ship. We wanted to go for appointments later on in the afternoon but she hadn't got any free spaces for another five days.'

'And we thought, goodness knows how many more people might have fatal accidents if we don't act pretty sharpish,' finished Mabel earnestly.

The Admiral nodded thoughtfully without speaking and took a long sip of his pint. Jimmy had managed to install the app Noah had described, but the Admiral had to admit, if only privately, that he was currently less than confident in its usage. Still, at least now he had the whole weekend to practice.

'Are we going to have a dummy run before then?' asked Jimmy almost reading the Admiral's mind.

'Not necessary Jimmy lad,' Charles Shackleford blustered self importantly. 'I've already mastered the damn thing. All Mabel and Emily have to do is put their ear pieces in and follow instructions. What could possibly go wrong…?'

Monday morning dawned and the Admiral was up and ready to go by seven thirty. He'd already taken Pickles out for a walk, an act which the spaniel didn't seem remotely grateful for if his refusal to take another step after he'd done his business was anything to go by. 'Bloody dog's spent too much time with Victory's mongrel,' the Admiral grumbled to himself, 'Getting soft in his old age.'

Nevertheless, he bent down to give his old canine friend a quick fuss before heading out of the kitchen to yell Mabel's name up the stairs. While he was waiting he fiddled with the iPad, to remind himself how to use it, then pulled a list of questions out of his pocket. Glancing down, he nodded in satisfaction. He was confident he'd covered every angle. He stuffed the questions back into his pocket and glanced down at his watch. Damn they were going to be late.

'MABEL,' he bellowed for the second time in exasperation, before sitting resignedly at the bottom of the stairs and staring at the classic oak panelling around him. You'd think the bloody woman would appreciate what he had to offer and make an honest man of him. After all, the Admiralty was a classic Edwardian building filled to bursting with antiques that would make the average American swoon – but did she appreciate it? No. Called it a draughty pile of bricks. The Admiral sighed. Sometimes he thought he'd never understand women.

'MABEL,' he roared for the third time, 'For God sake get your arse in gear woman, I'm going to have to park half a bloody mile away at this rate.'

'It really isn't necessary to shout Charlie,' answered Mabel tightly, limping down the stairs.

'What the bloody hell's wrong with you?' Charles Shackleford muttered, staring at her hobbling form in bewilderment.

'Emily advised that I should shave my legs seeing as I was having a pedicure and not a leg wax,' Mabel responded stiffly, walking past him, 'So I decided to borrow your razor.'

'You might have been better off using an industrial strimmer,' the Admiral responded, dubiously eying the wads of toilet paper dotting each shin.

Mabel stopped so suddenly, the Admiral bumped into her back. 'Not another word Charlie. Not one,' she said crisply without turning round. 'Not if you don't want to spend the rest of the week sharing a basket with Pickles.'

No, he really didn't understand women...

Luckily, they were still early enough to get straight on to the car ferry. Jimmy and Emily were meeting them for a last-minute briefing and a bacon sandwich once they'd managed to park the car.

Fate was definitely smiling on them as the Admiral slotted into a parking space less than fifty yards from the front of Birdie's Groom Room. 'Right then Mabel old girl,' he said, climbing laboriously out of the driver's seat, 'We've just got time to make sure we're all singing from the same hymn sheet, then it's up to you and Emily to conduct a successful undercover operation. He took her arm and opened the door to the small café in the covered market. 'All you both have to do is follow my lead and ask the questions I tell you to ask. Simple. We'll have the merry widow singing like a canary in no time.

'Now, do you fancy some black pudding on your bacon sandwich?'

CHAPTER 5

'Right then, put these ear plugs in and I can hear everything you say.'

'Before we go any further,' Jimmy said seriously, 'I feel I must remind everyone of some ground rules. We need to be extremely careful about what questions we ask.' He frowned and shook his head. 'I'm beginning to have second thoughts about this.'

'Bloody hell Jimmy, a bit late to start getting cold feet,' the Admiral said tetchily, handing the small pieces of plastic to Mabel and Emily. 'And anyway, what if we're right? What if Birdie Bennett actually put paid to old Barney?'

Jimmy sighed in resignation, then, after a short pause, pulled himself up, saying sternly, 'We just need to get a couple of things straight Sir, in case things get out of hand.' He pivoted in his seat and stared sombrely at his three companions, one at a time. Even though it was a bit unexpected, the Admiral had to admit the stare was very effective and thought he'd definitely give it a try when he needed to use The Look.

'We are not, and I mean *not*, under any circumstances to ask whether she offed her second husband. Do I make myself clear? We are not at this moment in time looking for a confession.'

The Admiral opened his mouth to argue, seeing as Jimmy's stipulation cancelled out half the questions on the paper in his pocket, but his old friend had put his Master At Arms hat on like he did at the Two Bridges and the Admiral found himself closing his mouth and nodding his head.

'Right then ladies,' the small man continued, 'I think it's time for your treatments.'

'Operation *A Flea in your Ear* is a go,' added the Admiral enthusiastically, putting his own earphones and microphone in place.

The two matrons got out of the car, fiddling with their ear pieces. 'Don't worry Mabel,' Emily muttered to her anxious friend as they tottered up the road, 'This is just another of the old goat's idiot ideas.'

'*I heard that.*' The Admiral's voice came over loud and clear and Mabel gave a small scream.

Thirty seconds later they disappeared into Birdie's Groom Room and the Admiral turned to Jimmy excitedly. 'Do you want to have a listen?'

'Good morning ladies,' Birdie trilled pleasantly as they shut the door behind them.

'*Say good morning,*' the Admiral's voice boomed in their ears, causing both ladies to jump.

Birdie smiled at them understandingly. 'Is this your first time in a beauty salon ladies?' she asked taking their coats. 'You have nothing to worry about, you can just lie back and enjoy it. Now who's going first?'

Emily and Mabel looked at each other. '*You go first Mabel.*'

'You go first Mabel,' Emily repeated with an encouraging look at her friend. They were getting the hang of this.

Five minutes later Mabel was ensconced in a large leather chair with her feet in a whirlpool of warm water. 'Ooh I say,' she said breathlessly, 'It tickles doesn't it?' Birdie laughed as she fetched her box of implements and sat at Mabel's feet. 'Would you like a magazine while you're waiting Emily?' she asked over her shoulder.

'Ask her how long she's lived in Dartmouth and why she decided to move here?'

'How long have you lived in Dartmouth?' asked Emily dutifully,

'And why did she... err... you, decide to move here?' added Mabel.

Birdie sighed, picking up Mabel's left foot and laying in into her lap. 'I moved here about five years ago,' she murmured, massaging Mabel's big toe, 'It was an impulsive decision, but one I've never regretted, even when I lost dear Barney.'

'Was he her first husband?'

'Was Barney your first husband?' Emily asked, 'I mean, I notice you have a daughter.'

'Bloody good question,'

'Thank you.'

'Sorry?'

'Err... thank you for letting us come to your lovely salon.'

'Ask her about the bloody daughter,'

'Oh be quiet,'

'I haven't said anything.'

' So, err... back to your... err... lovely daughter?'

'She certainly is a treasure,' Birdie Bennett's affection didn't appear unfeigned. 'Her father was my first husband, but he died in a terrible yachting accident when Angela was only fourteen.'

'Oh dear, that's dreadful,' murmured Mabel vaguely, her attention on the large razor blade Birdie had taken out of her box.

'To lose two husbands, such terribly bad luck,' Emily added, leaning forward to see what the beautician was doing.

'I've actually had three husbands,' Birdie corrected sadly, slicing at the hard skin on Mabel's heel.

'Bingo,'

'BINGO,' shouted Mabel as the razor blade reached a tender spot.

Birdie looked up in confusion. 'You were saying?' Emily insisted from behind her.

Another sigh. 'My second husband died in a fall just two years after we were married. It was so hard - on Angela especially. She was very close to Mike, and to lose two people she loved within just a few years... well, I'm just glad we still have each other. Goodness me your toe nails are strong Mabel.'

'She normally needs an angle grinder,'

'Shut up,'

'Oh I'm so sorry Mabel, that was a little insensitive of me. Would you like a cup of tea before I move on to your other foot?'

'That would be lovely dear, thank you.'

'How about you Emily, do you fancy a cuppa while you're waiting?'

At Emily's nod, Birdie headed through to the kitchen leaving the two matrons alone.

Ask her what her second husband did for a living and what his surname was.

'Such a terrible tragedy to have three husbands die in such unfortunate circumstances,' Emily murmured when Birdie came back with their tea.

'More than anyone should have to bear,' the beautician agreed sadly, taking the industrial clippers to the toe nails on Mabel's right foot.

'What did your second husband do for a living?' grunted Mabel as the clippers did their work.

'He had a hotel on the Isle of Wight,' wheezed Birdie, finally managing to cut the toe nail.

'Did he leave her the hotel when he popped his clogs?'

'I suppose you inherited the hotel when your husband had his unfortunate fall. Such a large inheritance must have made things a little easier for you and Angela.' Emily winced at Mabel's direct question, but Birdie didn't seem to mind.

'It did,' she agreed, 'Although nothing could make up for the loss of my dear Michael, I was able to sell up and start afresh here in Dartmouth.'

'What was his surname?'

'You do have a lovely house here in Dartmouth. It's on Lucius Street isn't it?'

'That's right,' Birdie responded, pulling the plug on the bowl of water and placing both Mabel's feet into a fluffy towel on her lap. 'I absolutely adore it, I'm not sure I could ever leave.' She rubbed Mabel's feet vigorously. 'Luckily Barney loved it too, so he was happy to move in with Angela and me.'

'What was her second husband's surname?'

'Didn't it get a spread in *South West Beautiful Homes* magazine?' Emily continued curiously.

Birdie nodded. 'Shall we do that nice bright pink on your toes Mabel?'

'I saw the pictures, it certainly does you credit dear.'

'Ask her about her husband's surname?'

'Perhaps you remember our house being used in a romantic comedy a couple of years ago?' Mabel asked with pride. 'The film was called *The Bridegroom*. It was very successful.'

'Of course I remember,' Birdie responded with a smile, 'Who could forget all that excitement. I took Angela to see the movie. We both loved it.

'Could you go into the cubicle in the back to take off your trousers Emily? There's a dressing gown you can slip on.' The beautician bent her head to finish painting Mabel's toe nails.

'What was her bloody husband's surname?'

'I'm sure your house is every bit as lovely dear,' offered Emily as she disappeared into the small back room.

'How did you meet Barney?' Mabel asked hesitantly as Birdie placed her feet in a portable dryer.

'We know how she bloody met him, ask about the bollocking surname...'

'It was up at the Naval College. We both went to the summer ball,' Birdie answered with a sigh.

'What about your second husband? Where did you meet him?' Mabel asked

'About bloody time.'

Birdie paused and stood up, picking her box of equipment off the floor. 'I can't really remember to be honest,' she said vaguely at length. 'I think we may have met at a club or something.'

'WHAT WAS HIS BOLLOCKING SURNAME?'

Mabel jumped and yelled, 'WHAT WAS HIS BOLLOCKING SURNAME?'

There was a silence as Birdie stared at the elderly matron in astonishment.

'Oh, don't worry about her,' Emily said coming back into the salon, 'I was hoping she'd behave herself, but I suppose it was too much to ask for.' She patted Birdie's hand. 'It's such a shame, but she has a rare form of Courgette's Syndrome. Now, where do you want me?'

CHAPTER 6

'So what have we found out?' the Admiral said leaning affectedly against the white board he'd set up in his office.

The other three looked at him in silence, then, sighing, Jimmy offered, 'Well, Birdie's second husband's surname was Wellington...'

'As in the boot,' offered the Admiral helpfully before waving Jimmy to continue.

'Mr. Wellington apparently died from some kind of fall after they'd been married for about two years.'

'That's a bit suspicious,' Emily commented darkly, 'I mean who's to say he wasn't pushed?'

'Good point well made Emily,' the Admiral said, pointing his felt tip pen towards her before turning round and writing, *Was he pushed?* on the white board.

'Shouldn't we write his name?' asked Mabel when he'd finished, 'I mean in case we forget it?' The Admiral sighed and crossed out *he*, replacing it with *Michael Wellington*. 'Carry on Jimmy.'

'Apparently Michael Wellington was the wealthy owner of a hotel on the Isle of Wight,' Jimmy continued. 'As his widow, Birdie inherited everything he owned, so she sold up, came to Dartmouth and bought both a house and a business, presumably with her second husband's money.'

'But what about husband number one?' asked Emily with a frown. 'We don't know how wealthy he was do we? Birdie could be some kind of black widow.'

'Well if she was, she dropped a bollock when she picked up Barney,' the Admiral commented bluntly, 'He hadn't got a pot to piss in. A bit of a gambler was our Mr. Bennett.'

Jimmy frowned. 'You'd have thought he had money though. I mean he used to flash it around a lot – always buying everyone drinks at that club he went to, always on holiday somewhere exotic. And what about that ridiculous sports car? He used to tear round here like he was on Brands Hatch circuit. Apparently he was driving it when he had his accident. The general consensus is that's how he damn well killed himself. Probably took the slip road too quickly and lost control.'

'But we know better,' the Admiral muttered thoughtfully.

'We don't really Sir,' disagreed Jimmy. 'All we have is an unfounded suspicion because (a) Birdie didn't go with him on the night he died and (b) he put off a visit to his mother's on that same night. I hate to say it Sir, but that's pretty much it.'

'Could Birdie have been worried about Barney spending all her money?' asked Emily astutely. 'Perhaps she thought he was rich when she agreed to marry him, but if she did, she must have been brought down to earth pretty sharpish.'

'I think we need some kind of timeline,' Jimmy said suddenly. 'Do you mind if I take over for a second Sir?' he asked standing up.

The Admiral hesitated then grudgingly handed over the felt tip pen.

Jimmy drew a circle at the top of the board. 'Here we have Marcus Tennant – Birdie's first husband. We don't know yet how long they were married, where they lived, or whether Mr. Tennant was wealthy,' he said, writing all three questions down next to the circle.

'I think we can assume he wasn't exactly penniless because he fell overboard on a yacht he owned. We also know that the accident happened during the Cowes Regatta – another indication that he was pretty well heeled.

'The accident happened when he was forty-six and Birdie was thirty eight. They had one daughter, Angela, aged fourteen. At this stage we don't know whether Birdie was the sole beneficiary of her husband's will.'

Jimmy paused and turned round. 'Have I missed anything so far Sir?' he asked the Admiral. Charles Shackleford shook his head and waved his former Master At Arms to continue.

Jimmy nodded and drew a line down to another circle.

'This is Birdie's second husband, Michael Wellington. We know he was the wealthy owner of a hotel on the Isle of Wight.' He turned back to his rapt audience. 'Which is of course where the Cowes Regatta takes place every year - so perhaps Birdie was already living there when she met Michael.'

He turned back to the board. 'Anyway, Birdie told Mabel and Emily that she'd been married to Michael for two years when he died. She then came pretty much straight to Dartmouth and she's been here for five years. That means she must have married Michael Wellington seven years ago, which, according to that newspaper article, was less than a year after her first husband died.' There was a collective gasp behind him.

'Well old Marcus hadn't been juggling halos very long, that's for sure,' was the Admiral's only comment. Jimmy nodded his head in agreement but didn't speak for a few seconds.

'So, Michael died just two years into their marriage in some kind of fall.' He turned round again, adding, 'History repeating itself?'

'We don't know how old he was or whether he had any children. We know he left everything to Birdie, but was there a first wife? Birdie intimated that her daughter adored her second husband, but we can't be sure if that was the case.'

'That seems pretty bloody unlikely to me, the Admiral interrupted, 'Seeing as her mother got hitched again before her dad was even cold.'

'But she was less than fifteen when her mother married Michael. That's a fairly vulnerable age and it's very likely she was looking for a father figure to replace the one she'd lost.

'So now we come to Barney. We're not sure how long they'd been married when he had his car accident, but we know it was definitely less than five years. They apparently met at a summer ball.

'It could be that Birdie was under the misapprehension that her third husband was a wealthy man – a fact which she had to have been disabused of fairly early on in their marriage. At this stage we don't know what kind of a relationship Barney had with his stepdaughter.

'We know that Birdie was supposed to have accompanied Barney on the night he died but cried off due to a migraine. We also know that Barney was supposed to have visited his mother before going on to Exeter. Is it coincidence that she lived on a road so steep, it would challenge the brakes of even the safest of cars?'

Jimmy placed the felt tip in a tray at the bottom of the white board and turned round to his audience again as he finished.

'So there you have it. Three men have died in mysterious circumstances. Is Birdie Bennett a Black Widow, or is she just a very unfortunate woman to have lost three husbands in extremely tragic circumstances?'

There was a few seconds silence then the Admiral stood up and patted the small man on the back. 'You've hit the nail right on the head Jimmy lad, I couldn't have put it better myself.'

∞∞∞

They finally discovered the gruesome details of Michael Wellington's death, and it didn't make very pretty reading.

Coincidentally, the accident happened pretty close to their neck of the woods, about ten miles away during a family weekend in Totnes in early May.

Michael had taken Birdie and Angela to visit Berry Pomeroy Castle, a large pile of romantic ruins, owned at one point by Edward Seymour, the first Duke of Somerset and Lord Protector of the Realm after Henry the Eighth's death in fifteen forty-seven.

Apparently, on the day they visited the weather had been awful, but not quite bad enough to close the castle. That said, the rain kept most of the tourists away, so Michael, Birdie and Angela had the site pretty much to themselves. A keen photographer, Michael had apparently revelled in it, delighting in the brooding atmosphere created by the inclement weather.

At about two thirty pm, Birdie had apparently had enough and decided to go and wait in the car. Angela joined her about half an hour later, supposedly leaving Michael clambering about happily.

According to the newspaper sources of the time, the rain finally stopped around three thirtyish and Birdie went back inside to see if she could hurry her husband along a bit, but despite looking everywhere, she could find no trace of him.

The police were called and Michael's body was eventually found in the bottom of a ravine near to the North-east tower.

Evidently he'd decided to try and get one last picture before the site closed for the day. In doing so, he'd somehow leaned too far over the crumbling wall facing out onto the steep sided valley and fallen to his death on the rocks below. There were no witnesses, and a verdict of accidental death was recorded.

The pictures taken at the time of Michael's death showed both Birdie and Angela drawn, pale and apparently wracked with grief. It was difficult to imagine that either had had anything to do with Michael's death. Angela especially took it badly, refusing to leave her room, even to go to school.

It wasn't hard to see why Birdie decided to take her daughter and start afresh, though why she chose to live within spitting distance of her husband's demise remained a mystery.

Nevertheless, on the face of it, a distraught widow and a teenage step-daughter ravaged by grief.

And Charles Shackleford didn't believe a word of it...

CHAPTER 7

The Admiral was under cover. Operation *Have a Shufti* had been underway for just over ten minutes.

He had to admit it had been harder than he'd thought to convince Jimmy of the necessity to have a clandestine look around Birdie Bennett's home, given that his former Master At Arms didn't have a very high opinion of breaking and entering. For a few nail-biting seconds Charles Shackleford believed he'd have to carry out *Have a Shufti* as a lone operative.

Thankfully though, when he pointed out to Jimmy the importance of having back-up, the small man had capitulated and was even now waiting in the car round the corner with his headset and microphone in place.

The Admiral looked around furtively, putting on his hard hat. He was currently dressed as a builder courtesy of Victory's friend Freddy who'd earlier taken part in a tribute to *The Village People*. It had to be said that the t-shirt was a trifle tight, and he wasn't impressed with the large Y.M.C.A logo plastered across the back of his denim over-shirt. The trousers were also a smidgeon too small and if he bent over too quickly, he'd very likely give everyone behind him a full view of his credentials. He'd initially refused to wear them until Mabel had assured him that builder's bottom was a necessary requirement of any tradesman worth his salt.

'I'm in position,' he whispered to Jimmy after making sure his ear piece was secure, then he turned and tiptoed down the steps leading to Birdie's back door.

Jimmy was sweating despite the coolness of the day. How the bloody hell did he always get himself into these situations?

At first, he'd categorically refused to take part in the Admiral's latest harebrained idea, citing the simple fact that breaking and entering was against the law. Of course he'd tried the old, 'You'll be disgraced for the rest of your life Sir,' and, 'Think about Tory and the baby Sir,' not to mention, 'Think of your position Sir,' tactics, but everything he said had been like water off a duck's back and he was reminded once again that Charles Shackleford didn't give a flying fig what anyone else thought about him.

Even, 'You could go to prison - again,' had merely elicited, 'Only if we get caught Jimmy lad...' And it was that statement, together with the excited gleam in the Admiral's eyes that had convinced Jimmy that he couldn't allow his former commanding officer to go it alone. He just took comfort from the hope that the Admiral's blithe, 'Everybody leaves a spare key out somewhere round the back door,' was, in this instance completely off the mark. As far as he could remember, Charles Shackleford didn't include lock picking as one of his skills.

'Are you reading me Jimmy lad, over?'

Jimmy sighed and answered, Reading you loud and clear Sir, over.'

'I'm at the back door now, and am looking for the key, over.'

'Keep me posted Sir, over and out.'

Jimmy could hear the Admiral grunting and muttering as he searched under the door mat, strategically placed plant pots, the underside of the window sill and finally any and all large stones within a thirty yard radius of the back door. His hopes rose as the Admiral's muttering became more colourful.

'Have you found the key Sir, over?' Jimmy whispered, unable to contain himself any longer.

'Negative, over,' came the Admiral's irritable reply. Jimmy breathed a sigh of relief, expecting the large man to appear round the corner any moment. After five minutes, when he didn't materialize, Jimmy felt a sinking in the pit of his stomach.

'Sir, are you there Sir, over?'

'I'm here Jimmy lad, over,' came Charles Shackleford's wheezing response after a few heart stopping seconds.

'What are you doing Sir?' Jimmy whispered, forgetting to add, 'Over,' in his agitation.

'There's... a... bathroom... window... open..., over.' The Admiral's voice this time was interspersed with puffing and panting, and Jimmy realized with dismay that his old friend was trying to climb through the window. 'Sir, stop. You'll get stuck Sir, he hissed as loudly as he dared, 'Please don't do anything foolish Sir.' There was an ominous cracking sound followed by a thump. Jimmy felt panic rise into his throat. 'OH MY GOD, YOU'VE BROKEN THE BOLLOCKING WINDOW CHARLIE,' he yelled, completely forgetting about the need for silence.

There was no response for a few seconds and Jimmy sat with his heart in his mouth, straining to hear what was happening. After about half a minute, he heard scuffling, then the gasping voice of his former commanding officer came through his earphones.

'Don't worry Jimmy lad, I'm right as rain,' over.'

'Where are you Sir, over?' Jimmy whispered back, struggling to contain his anxiety.

'I'm inside Jimmy lad,' the Admiral rasped with barely restrained excitement, 'Just landed on a bollocking vase that's all. Bloody ugly thing it was, she'll be glad to be rid of it I'm sure, over.'

'You can't just leave bits of china all over the floor Sir, over.'

'Well there's lots of water and a few flowers too, so she'll probably think the cat did it, over.'

Jimmy groaned. 'We have no idea if she's got a bloody cat Sir. You need to clean up the mess, over.' There was no response.

'Sir, Sir… SIR.' Jimmy could hear footsteps.

'I'm just having a shufti upstairs,' the Admiral whispered finally, 'I'll let you know if I find anything, over and out…'

Jimmy pulled off his headgear and flung it on the seat next to him in frustration. This was the last time, the absolute bollocking LAST TIME he ever got caught up in Charles Shackleford's foolhardy, reckless, madcap, not to mention half baked, bloody idiotic ideas. He stared at the roof of the car, trying to get his anger under control, then finally sighed. Maybe now was the right time to give Emily's mindfulness exercises a go.

'Jimmy, Jimmy can you hear me, over?' The Admiral's voice came from the headphones on the seat. Resignedly, Jimmy leaned over and picked them up.

'I hear you Sir, over,' he responded flatly.

'What's got into you Jimmy?' the Admiral responded with an audible frown, 'You sound like a fart in a trance, over.'

'I'm fine Sir,' Jimmy responded through gritted teeth. 'Do you have anything to report, over?'

'I've found something Jimmy lad,' Charles Shackleford murmured. 'There's a photo on old Birdie's dressing table. It's of her first husband Marcus standing on his yacht Tempest. It's dated the day before he popped his clogs. And get this,' he added gleefully, 'Old Michael's on it too. They're laughing together.'

'So Birdie's first two husbands knew each other, it looks like they could even have been friends. But that's not the best bit Jimmy boy.' The Admiral took a deep breath and let it out in an excited rush before finishing, 'It looks as though her second husband could have been on the yacht when her first husband fell overboard…'

Jimmy felt his excitement mount, despite his misgivings. 'What makes you think Michael was on the yacht when Marcus was killed?'

'Because they're both wearing exactly the same yachting clobber, obviously belonging to the same crew. They were racing in the Cowes Regatta together.'

Jimmy was silent for a second, taking in this latest development.

'So are you thinking what I'm thinking Jimmy lad?'

'Was Birdie having an affair with Michael? And could he have pushed Marcus overboard?' Jimmy answered promptly.

'Exactly,' the Admiral responded animatedly. 'I'll just take a couple of shots of this picture, then I'll get out of here.'

'Be careful Sir, over and out,' responded Jimmy, his weariness replaced with newly fired enthusiasm.

Well that was an unexpected turn up for the books and no mistake, Jimmy reflected. He wasn't sure if it got them any closer to finding Barney's potential murderer, but it really was beginning to look as though that might be the tip of the iceberg.

Suddenly out of the corner of his eye, he saw a car pass on his left and put on its indicator to turn the corner. He drew his breath sharply. It was Birdie. He glanced down at his watch. She was two hours early.

'Sir, Sir, are you there Sir, over?'

'What's wrong now Jimmy, over?' The Admiral's irritated response quickly changed as Jimmy hissed, 'Birdie's back. Abort the mission, I repeat abort the mission, over.'

'Bollocking bollocks,' muttered the Admiral, 'I'm buggered.'

Jimmy clambered out of his car, holding onto the iPad for dear life. For a second his brain refused to function, then he slammed the door and hurried after Birdie's car as it disappeared round the corner.

'You need to get out through the back door before she parks the car,' Jimmy barked, not bothering to keep his voice down.

'Roger that,' the Admiral puffed, heading to the landing. Operation *Have a Shufti* had never been so precarious.

Jimmy could hear the large man thundering down the stairs as he turned the corner and skidded to a halt. Heart in his mouth, he watched Birdie get out of her car, then go round to the boot to take out some shopping. Jimmy took a deep breath then began walking towards her, not sure what he intended to do, but knowing he had to employ some kind of delaying tactic.

'Where are you Sir?' he asked shortly, his *over* having gone completely out.

There was no answer. Through the headphones he heard the back door slam at exactly the same time as Birdie's car boot.

'Excuse me, Mrs. Bennett?' he called, pulling off his head gear and hurrying towards the widow as she turned and paused.

Out of the corner of his eye, Jimmy saw the gate open behind her but kept his focus fully on Birdie Bennett.

'I just wanted to offer my condolences on the death of your husband,' Jimmy offered breathlessly when he was a couple of yards away.

'That's very kind of you, Mr....?' Birdie put her bags of shopping down and took a few steps forward, smiling with just the right amount of sadness. As he took her hand, Jimmy couldn't help but wonder if it was a complete charade.

'N...Noon,' Jimmy admitted, seeing no advantage in lying. 'I knew Barney from his time in the Navy. We'd lost touch in recent years, but when I heard he'd died so tragically, I just had to come and say how sorry I am for your loss. Barney was a good man.' And it was true, he was.

Behind her Jimmy could see the Admiral quietly ease the gate shut and tiptoe painstakingly up the steps towards Birdie's car parking space. His hard hat had slipped rakishly towards the side and his trousers were in danger of getting him arrested for indecent exposure. Just as he reached the pavement, something must have alerted the widow and she turned, dropping Jimmy's hand with a start.

'Oh you're early,' she exclaimed, 'I wasn't expecting you until twelve. Still, now you're here you might as well go and make a start while I make you a cup of tea. I know how you builders like a regular brew.'

She turned back to Jimmy with another smile. 'Please excuse me Mr. Noon, I thought I had another half an hour before the builder arrived, and I have to put my shopping away. She gave a small grimace, leaning forward and whispering, 'Now he's here, I don't want to keep him waiting, after all, time is money and you know what builders are like, I need to make sure he knocks the correct wall down. I'm sure you understand...'

CHAPTER 8

The look of panic on the Admiral's face would have been comical had things not been so serious. Nevertheless, Charles Shackleford had the foresight to mutter, 'Be right wiv yer missus,' as Birdie headed down the steps.

'Bollocks,' he hissed to Jimmy as the widow went through the gate, 'What the bloody hell am I going to do now?'

'OH TIGGER YOU'RE SUCH A NAUGHTY CAT, LOOK WHAT YOU'VE DONE TO MUMMY'S VASE...' Birdie's shout reached them both just as a large van pulled up beside them sporting the words, *Brian's Builders, no job too small.*

Both men turned in time to see a large bear of a man climb down from the driver's seat. He looked towards the Admiral with a frown. 'Ere, wot you up to sunshine? Hope yer not thinkin of musclin' in on my bloody job.'

The Admiral stared speechlessly as the man mountain approached them, lurid visions of a six-week stint in traction completely strangling his vocal cords.

Next to him, Jimmy took a strategic step backwards, muttering, 'I think it's time to scarper Sir…'

By the time they reached the car, Charles Shackleford's courage had reasserted itself and he had to admit, if only privately, that he was pretty ashamed of his lily livered response to Brian the Builder. So much so, that as they drove past Brian who was now unloading his van, the Admiral felt safe enough winding down the window and yelling, 'SCRUNTFUTTOCK,' at the top of his voice.

Obviously, he didn't expect the incredible hulk to actually chase after the car. It was a good job Jimmy had done a bit of stock car racing in his youth.

'Bloody hell that was close Jimmy lad,' the Admiral muttered as they drove back down Victoria Street.

'What on earth were you thinking?' Jimmy retorted heatedly, 'I'm sorry Sir, but sometimes I can't help but think you just go around looking for people to lamp you one. If that moron had caught up with us, we could have been pushing up daisies by the weekend.'

The Admiral snorted loudly. 'Don't be such a damn pansy Jimmy,' he responded, the whole incident already being remodelled in his head.

'Operation *Have a Shufti* needed an element of flexibility in its execution. There we were, on the verge of having to rebuild old Birdie's house, when Fred Flintstone poled up. So, like all the best plans, it was a self-adjusting cock up.'

Jimmy opened his mouth to respond but shut it again without speaking. What was the point? He knew to his cost that the Admiral's version of any event was usually more akin to a damn fairy tale than real life. Sighing, he slowed down to join the short line of cars waiting for the ferry.

'Get out of the queue Jimmy, quick.' The Admiral's urgent request along with an unexpected tug on his arm, brought Jimmy out of his reverie.

'What's wrong?' the small man asked, slamming his foot on the brake as sudden fear took hold. 'Desperate Dan's not followed us down here has he?' The Admiral cast him a scathing look and pointed across the road. Just going into the Floating Bridge Inn next to the ferry dock was Birdie's daughter Angela.

'Don't look now Jimmy lad, but I think our suspect is chatting up the barman.'

The two men were nursing a pint and a packet of crisps in the corner of the bar, keeping a close watch on their quarry. Or at least the Admiral was, Jimmy was keeping a pretty close watch on a fly hovering over the back of the Admiral's head.

'Don't you think we've done enough for one day Sir?' he asked with a sigh. 'I told Emily I'd be back for lunch. She's making cheese on toast,' he added a little plaintively.

'Stop whinging Jimmy,' was the Admiral's unsympathetic comment. 'You don't think Dick Tracy moaned about missing his cheese on bloody toast when he was on a case do you?'

Jimmy took another sip of his pint, knowing it was futile to argue further. Sometimes he couldn't help but fantasize about a life without Charles Shackleford in it.

'She's just leaned over and given the bloke a smacker,' observed the Admiral gleefully. 'Have you ever clocked him here before?'

'I don't know, I can't see him,' said Jimmy sulkily earning him The Look. 'Get a damn grip man,' the Admiral admonished him, 'You'll be on bloody dishwasher duty if you don't buck up.'

Sitting up straighter, Jimmy heaved another sigh and finally gave up any idea of lunch accompanied by *Bargain Hunt* on the telly. Taking another sip of his pint, he casually turned round until he was facing the bar. Initially looking everywhere but at the amorous couple, he slowly allowed his eyes to drift in their direction before turning back to face the Admiral.

'I'm not really sure,' was his helpful comment, 'I think the lad might have been here quite a while, but then again I could be wrong.'

The Admiral narrowed his eyes, wondering if his former Master At Arms was being flippant, but Jimmy's expression was anything but glib, in fact he was staring out of the window like he'd seen a ghost.

'What the bloody hell's wrong with you Jimmy?' the large man asked, 'You look like a lost fart in a haunted milk bottle.'

'I'm not sure if I'm seeing things Sir,' breathed Jimmy, 'But the chap coming into the pub now looks exactly like Marcus Tennant, Birdie's first husband. The one who fell off his yacht and drowned.'

The two men sat with bated breath as the newcomer entered the bar. 'Could it be him do you think?' Jimmy murmured nervously, not daring to turn round in case they drew attention to themselves.

The Admiral frowned and looked down at his mobile phone, bringing up the picture he'd taken earlier of Marcus Tennant. 'He certainly looks like him,' Charles Shackleford muttered, 'And he's walked straight over to Angela, so if he's not our man, then he's a very close relation.'

Taking a covering sip of his pint, the Admiral covertly watched the exchange between Birdie's daughter and the stranger. 'What's he doing?' hissed Jimmy impatiently after a few minutes.

'He's talking to the daughter,' the Admiral responded, 'But whatever they're chatting about, it's getting a bit bloody animated if their waving arms are anything to go by.' He shook his head in irritation. 'I just wish they'd speak up a bit.'

'What's the barman doing?' asked Jimmy curiously.

'He's standing staring at the two of them looking damn uncomfortable,' the Admiral answered, 'You know that look someone gets when they wish a hole would swallow them up?'

Jimmy nodded. 'I get that often,' he muttered dryly, earning him another narrow eyed look.

'We need to come up with a plan to find out if it really is Marcus Tennant, or his bloody doppelganger,' the Admiral continued.

'How?' asked Jimmy shrugging his shoulders. 'It's not like we can ask him to give a sample of his DNA.'

The Admiral sat in silence for a few moments, watching as the lively exchange came to an end. As he stared, Angela leaned up to give the tall man a quick kiss on the cheek while the barman pulled him a pint.

'Right Jimmy,' Charles Shackleford finally said, before finishing his own beer and placing it decisively on the table, 'Let's see if we can catch the bastard out.' He stood up determinedly, then, leaned forward, ostensibly to finish his crisps.

'Follow my lead Jimmy lad,' he mumbled taking a mouthful. The small man had no time to protest as the Admiral stepped away from the table and walked resolutely towards the two people at the bar.

Heart thumping, Jimmy finished his pint and hurried after him, catching up just in time to hear the Admiral boom, 'Marcus Tennant, I haven't seen you for years. Heard you'd paid a visit to Davy Jones' locker. Just shows how wrong rumours can be.'

'Do I know you?' asked *Marcus* eying the Admiral's building contractor's get up dubiously.

'I should say so,' the Admiral bluffed, patting the man on the back jovially, 'Used to do a bit of sailing myself back in the day.'

'I think you have me confused with my brother,' the man said stiffly when the Admiral continued to stand grinning like a demented Cheshire cat.

'I know you,' Angela spoke up suddenly, having been silent until now. She looked Charles Shackleford up and down, her face radiating dislike, 'You're that weird bloody Admiral who came to Barney's funeral. The one who was asking mum a whole bunch of creepy questions.'

She leaned forward, thrusting her face in front of the Admiral's angrily. Charles Shackleford stepped back, the hyena grin faltering a little.

'What the hell do you want?' Angela spat out, 'And why are you dressed up like a navvy? Are you *following* me?' Her voice was loud and full of outrage. Jimmy couldn't tell if it was genuine or not, but, as they began attracting interest, he deemed it a good time for a strategic withdrawal.

'Following you?' the small man asked in a voice radiating bewilderment. 'We were just having a quick pint after my friend here spent the morning in his allotment.' He looked over at the Admiral who was nodding his head vigorously in agreement. 'I'm sorry if you found his remarks offensive, but to my knowledge, there's no law against simply speaking with somebody.' Then, without giving the Admiral a chance to bury them any deeper, he took the large man's arm and dragged him, still grinning inanely, towards the entrance.

'So, old Marcus had a brother,' the Admiral muttered as they hurried back to the car. 'I wonder what he's doing in Dartmouth?'

'Well he is Angela's uncle,' Jimmy responded brusquely, climbing into the driver's seat. 'I mean, he could be over to give his niece a bit of moral support after old Barney's accident. Perhaps even Birdie as well. Just because we suspect foul play in his brother's demise, doesn't mean he does.'

The Admiral frowned as they finally pulled onto the car ferry. 'Unless of course he had reason to want Marcus dead.'

'If we're not careful, we'll start spreading ourselves too thin,' Jimmy protested, shaking his head. 'I say we concentrate on the Michael Wellington angle for now. If we can prove he was having an affair with Birdie, then the police just might consider he had reason to toss

Marcus overboard. Don't forget Sir, our prime reason for getting involved in this whole affair was to find out if Barney Bennett was given a bit of a hand exiting this mortal coil.'

The Admiral nodded before turning to his friend excitedly. 'Bit of a turn up for the books though eh Jimmy? That's two leads we've uncovered today and you've not even had your cheese on toast yet.' Charles Shackleford rubbed his hands gleefully and continued, 'There's no doubt about it, we're cooking on gas Jimmy lad, we're cooking on bloody gas…'

Ten minutes later they pulled up outside the Admiralty. As his friend clambered out of the car, Jimmy couldn't help but wince at the sight that briefly hovered a mere foot from his nose and he gave thanks that the Admiral's regular attire generally included a pair of extra strong braces.

'Right, Jimmy lad,' Charles Shackleford said, sticking his head back into the car. 'We'll reconvene here tomorrow morning at Oh nine hundred hours on the dot.'

'Yes Sir.' Jimmy didn't dare disagree when the Admiral started using military timing.

'In the meantime get Emily to have a shufti on that bloody pill of hers and goggle old Marcus's brother, see if we can come up with a name.'

'It's called a Tablet Sir,' Jimmy corrected just as the Admiral slammed the door, so hard, the car alarm went off. Sighing, the small man started the engine and slowly turned the car around, mulling over the events of the morning.

Despite his misgivings, he couldn't help feeling a small bubble of excitement. While going along with the Admiral's harebrained schemes didn't make for an easy life, Jimmy had to concede, if only to himself, that it was never boring either.

CHAPTER 9

Marcus's brother turned out to have the unenviable name of Norbert, and the reason they looked so similar was because the two men had actually been twins.

'Bloody hell, he drew the short straw,' commented the Admiral when Emily self-importantly informed him of her findings. 'Jimmy's right, we can't spread ourselves too thinly, but we do need to keep tabs on him. I mean, if my parents called me Norbert and my brother Marcus, that would be enough in itself to make me want to do him in.'

'And don't forget the daughter,' added Emily, in full Mata Hari mode.

They'd reconvened this time in the Admiralty kitchen so that Mabel could keep an eye on her flapjacks, obviously with the enthusiastic help of Pickles.

Emily had also discovered that Norbert was an insurance salesman who still lived in the house that had belonged to his parents in Fareham – a mere stone's throw across the water from the Isle of Wight, affectionately known to its residents as Dinosaur Island.

'I think it's time for me and Jimmy to take a road trip,' stated the Admiral in a voice that brooked no arguments. 'We'll start in Fareham, then head over to the Isle of Wight and see if we can find anyone who remembers any hanky panky going on between Birdie and Michael.'

'What are we going to do?' asked Mabel anxiously.

'Keep tabs on our suspects in Dartmouth,' the Admiral offered gravely. He leaned forward conspiratorially. 'Mabel it's your job to keep an eye on old Birdie. The easiest way to do that will be to treat yourself to a few more *procedures* at Birdie's Groom Room. Perhaps you could have one of those face lift thingies. Anyway, it's up to you, whatever you fancy my dove. I'll leave you a tenner…'

The Admiral turned to Emily. 'It's up to you to keep tabs on Angela. She seems to be a bit of a feisty piece of work so you won't want to get too close. Try and find out where she works, who her friends are, that sort of thing. And most importantly, how did she get on with Barney?'

Emily nodded, already mentally revamping her wardrobe in true private investigator style. 'What about Norbert?' she asked, wondering how they were going to keep an eye on the elusive brother. The Admiral looked over at Jimmy and gave him a nod.

'At this stage we're only interested in him as far as his relationships with Birdie and Angela go,' the small man commented seriously. 'By keeping an eye on those two, we should be able to spot if there's anything untoward going on involving a third party.

'Now what you need to remember ladies, is tha ….' He was interrupted as the intercom for the outside gate buzzed loudly.

Irritably the Admiral got to his feet and went over to press the two way button. 'WHATEVER YOU WANT, WE'RE NOT BLOODY INTERESTED,' he shouted, and was just about to cut whoever it was off, when a hesitant male voice said, 'Is this the residence of Admiral Charles Shackleford?'

'WHAT OF IT?' the Admiral yelled back.

'My name's Joseph... Joseph Wellington. I'm Michael Wellington's son and I think I need your help...'

Looking over at the other three in astonishment, Charles Shackleford pressed the remote switch controlling the gate and went to open the front door.

The car that came through the gate had definitely seen better days and for a moment the Admiral wondered about the wisdom of letting a stranger in without any prior sight of his credentials. A couple of seconds later, however, all thoughts of identification went completely out of his head as the barman from the Floating Bridge got out of the car.

Five minutes later Joseph, 'Please call me Joe,' was ensconced at the kitchen table with a large plate of flapjacks in front of him.

'When you marched over calling Marcus Tennant's name and Angela said you'd been asking questions, I knew we needed to talk,' the young man said earnestly.

'Aren't you her boyfriend or something?' Jimmy asked suspiciously, 'Or is necking with the customers part of being a good barman nowadays?'

Joe reddened then stared back at Jimmy defiantly. 'My father fell to his death five years ago,' he said directly, 'But I don't believe it was an accident. I think my father was murdered.' His voice cracked slightly and he paused, twisting his fingers anxiously. 'Just like Marcus Tennant and now Barney Bennett.'

The ensuing silence was deafening, even the Admiral was for once at a complete loss for words. Eventually it was Mabel who spoke first. Leaning forward, she tapped the young man on his arm and said, 'Have a flapjack Joe.'

Her words broke the hiatus and the Admiral glanced over at Jimmy before saying brusquely, 'Well you can spout that load of bollocks all you like, but if you haven't got any proof, that's all it is, a load of old bollocks.'

'Who says I haven't got any proof?' Joe retorted sharply.

'Why haven't you gone to the police then?' Jimmy asked levelly.

The young man slumped in his chair. 'I have,' he muttered, 'But they're not interested.'

'So it's not proof then,' Jimmy insisted calmly. 'What exactly is it you want from us Mr. Wellington?'

'You were asking questions,' Joe persisted, 'And when I googled you, there was a story about how you solved a murder at some hotel on Dartmoor.' He leant down and rummaged inside a holdall he'd brought in with him, eventually pulling out a large envelope. 'I received this letter from my father,' he murmured, placing the envelope on the table. 'Once you've had a look at it, I was hoping you'd be interested in helping me.'

∞∞∞

'I hadn't seen my father for three years before his death. When he and my mother split up, she took me to live with her parents in Cumbria. For the first two years she forbade me to have any contact with him.' Joe grimaced ruefully, 'It wasn't an amicable split as you can probably gather. My father...' he floundered.

'Had a great deal of difficulty keeping it in his y-fronts?' the Admiral suggested for him flatly.

Joe laughed humourlessly. 'Well that's one way of putting it I suppose. He was always popular with the ladies, but I know he cared about me.

'He used to send my mother endless letters – grovelling apologies really, together with continual entreaties to allow him to see me. She threw every one of them in the bin. I used to sneak down and steal them back when she was in bed.' He shook his head. 'It was pretty pathetic to be honest, but it proved to me that whatever had happened between him and my mother, he really did love me. So as soon as I turned sixteen, I went down to see him.

'I don't know what I expected. Maybe I thought we'd sail off into the sunset, father and son together and have lots of Indiana Jones type adventures.' He laughed harshly. 'I waited too long. By the time I arrived in the Isle of Wight, Birdie Tennant had already got her claws firmly embedded.'

'So, what happened?' breathed Emily nibbling on a flapjack.

'To say he was besotted would be an understatement,' Joe continued scathingly. 'She was married to Marcus but that didn't seem to stop either of them. It was so damn painful to watch,' he ground out venomously, 'It was like she had some kind of invisible string and he was her bloody puppet.

'Then I'd see him together with Marcus – laughing and joking. The stupid fool didn't seem to have a bloody inkling what was going on under his nose. Talk about blindness. I was sixteen for God's sake and I could see it.' He stopped and heaved a sigh, shaking his head.

'In the end, I left. He had no time for anyone but that woman. I went back up to Cumbria and my mother's, 'I told you so,' and twelve months later Marcus was dead.

'They didn't even wait a decent interval to get married. I was invited to the wedding but I couldn't bring myself to go, so I made an excuse.

'The next time I heard from my father was three months before he died. He said he had something he wanted to tell me. That was the letter he sent,' Joe added nodding towards the envelope on the table. 'It was long and meandering, like he was drunk or something. But in it he said that he couldn't live any longer knowing what she'd done. He didn't say who *she* was or what it was that she'd done, but I knew he meant Birdie.

'He asked if I'd meet with him.' The sadness in Joe's voice was unfeigned, and when he looked up, there were tears in his eyes. 'I was due to go travelling to Thailand the following week,' he murmured sadly, 'So I put him off, said I would see him when I got back.

'But when I got back, he was already dead.'

'What makes you think he was murdered?' Jimmy asked evenly.

'I think Birdie found out he intended to rat her out,' Joe responded, the Americanism giving away his youth. 'And I think she killed him before he got the chance.'

'Does Angela know who you are?' the Admiral asked. 'I can't imagine her willingly canoodling with you after you let her know you believed her mother was a double murderer.'

Joe shook his head. 'I told her my name was Tony,' he said with a shrug, 'That I was down for the summer season.'

'How come she didn't recognize you?' Jimmy asked dubiously.

'We never met,' was the simple reply. 'I only knew what she looked like from old photos my dad sent me.'

'So you haven't been in Dartmouth long then?' queried Mabel curiously.

Joe shook his head again. 'I came when I heard about Barney Bennett's death,' he responded, before continuing vehemently, 'It can't just be coincidence that three men married to the same woman all died in mysterious circumstances. I thought I might finally have a chance to find out what really happened to my father.'

'So you decided you'd start with Birdie's daughter,' the Admiral stated impassively. 'Bit callous wouldn't you say?'

'Not if you knew her,' Joe answered with a small shudder. 'She's a cold, calculating bitch. I can't believe I felt sorry for her all those years, even when I was jealous she had the father that should have been mine.

'I got to know her through the local sailing club. I knew she was a keen sailor, so I joined up. I'm not sure what I hoped to accomplish. I suppose I thought it would somehow get me closer to Birdie, but believe me, she might not show it to the world, but Angela hates her mother with a passion.'

'How do you know that?' asked Jimmy doubtfully.

'Because the last time I saw her before today, she offered me twenty thousand pounds to kill her.'

CHAPTER 10

'Are you sure you don't want me to drive Sir?' Jimmy asked as they swerved round a hairpin bend, only narrowly missing a cyclist who almost ended up in a ditch at the side of the road.

'Bloody road hog,' muttered the Admiral, ignoring the dwindling expletives yelled after them as the cyclist picked up his bike.

'You know it's better that I drive Jimmy lad,' he said when the irate figure finally disappeared out of the rear-view mirror. 'It would take us til next week to get to Fareham with you at the bloody wheel. I know you mean well Jimmy boy, but you drive like a bollocking pensioner.'

'I am a pensioner,' responded Jimmy through gritted teeth, 'And I hate to surprise you Sir, but so are you.'

'What do you think to Joe Wellington's story?' the Admiral asked, hastily changing the subject.

Jimmy shrugged. 'I'm not sure to be honest Sir. He seems kosher enough, but we've only got his word for it that he is who he says he is. Mind you, the letter from his father looked genuine.'

The Admiral nodded. 'I can't think of a good reason why he'd be wasting his time telling a load of porkies to us unless Birdie and Angela put him up to it.' He looked over at Jimmy, 'Trying to suss out what we know.'

Jimmy gripped the sides of his seat and shut his eyes as the Admiral veered into the middle of the road. 'Please keep your eyes on the road Sir,' he pleaded.

Muttering under his breath, the Admiral turned back to the road ahead and for a few minutes they were silent.

'I hardly think Angela would offer to pay him to finish off her mother, then tell him to spy on us at the same time,' Jimmy finally offered with a frown. 'Sounds too much like James Bond to be true. In fact that's the bit that I'm having the most trouble with.' He turned towards the Admiral. 'If Angela's offered him money to get rid of Birdie, why hasn't he made any effort to get it on tape? Surely that would be enough to give the police an excuse to investigate into Barney's death at the bloody least.'

'Could be he's just scared,' the Admiral responded with a shrug, 'Or he thinks she's bluffing. I mean it's not a regular request from a new girlfriend is it?'

'Anyway, for the time being, he's said he'll keep tabs on the uncle via Angela and try to hold off her murdering instincts until we get back.'

'And he's given us some Intel that might be useful,' Jimmy added. 'We now know where Birdie and Marcus were living when he went over the side, and we know the name of the sailing club all three of them belonged to.'

'He didn't seem to know a great deal about Norbert Tennant though did he?' reflected the Admiral. 'Although he seemed to think that Angela was as surprised as he was to see her uncle in Dartmouth. I wonder if Angela was close to her uncle when her father was alive?'

mused Jimmy, 'Could be he wasn't on the scene much, living in Fareham instead of the Isle of Wight.

'Still, Joe's story proves one more thing. Old Marcus Tennant must have been fairly loaded or he wouldn't have been living on Dinosaur Island. I wonder what old Norbert thought about that?'

Three hours later they turned off the Motorway and headed into Fareham town centre. The afternoon traffic was starting to build up and they wanted to get this bit of Operation *Murderous Marriages* over with as quickly as possible so they could head over to Portsmouth harbour before it got too late and be ready for the ferry across to the Isle of Wight first thing in the morning.

'Have you got that Sat Nav thing on properly Jimmy?' asked the Admiral after they'd gone round the town centre for the third time. 'I'm beginning to get bloody dizzy.'

'It keeps re-calculating the damn route,' Jimmy responded in frustration. 'The house must be somewhere near here.'

Ten minutes later they were finally parked outside a large Victorian terraced house that looked as though it had seen better days. Clambering out of the car, the Admiral stared up at the ornate façade.

'Looks a bit dejected doesn't it?' he said with a frown. 'If I were a betting man Jimmy lad, I'd take ten to one this place hasn't been lived in for months.'

An elderly neighbour told them the house was due to go to auction at the end of May. 'Mr. Tennant, the owner has fallen on hard times.' She leaned forward and whispered the last bit, all the while looking furtively around as if she was afraid the gossip monster would suddenly appear and snatch her down into the bowels of hell.

'He's been very sick, poor man. Not physical you understand, but sort of a mental thing.' She tapped the side of her head to make sure they got the message. 'He had a breakdown six months ago and we haven't seen him since.'

'Mad as a box of frogs you mean,' clarified the Admiral bluntly. The elderly neighbour coloured up and spluttered that she wouldn't call him *that* exactly, but in her opinion he was definitely a sandwich short of a picnic...

It took them another fifteen minutes to convince her they didn't need to know the life history and mental state of everyone else living on the road, and they only managed to finally get away when the Admiral mentioned that he'd love to stay and chat, but a recurring bout of Dengue fever meant that he couldn't be around people for too long, 'Just in case...'

∞∞∞

Joe Wellington was a troubled young man. He'd come to Dartmouth to finally solve the riddle of his father's untimely demise. The letter he received from Michael had haunted him since he'd returned from Thailand and the guilt for not being there when his father needed him was getting stronger day by day.

But in the month he'd been here, the only thing he'd managed to achieve was the involvement of a bunch of eccentric geriatrics who thought they were bang smack in the middle of an Agatha Christie novel. His visit to the Admiral's house and subsequent discloser of his father's admittedly vague suspicions had only served to complicate matters.

Joe was convinced that somehow Birdie was responsible for his father's death. It was the only answer that made sense. But despite his best efforts, Angela had so far given nothing away apart from the fact that she loathed her mother. He still wasn't sure whether her request had been a macabre joke or not. And even if it was, it was a bit disconcerting that she was so ready to believe him capable of killing someone. Maybe his playacting had been too good, or perhaps murderous tendencies simply ran in their family. He shook his head in confusion, unsure whether he should have gone to the police.

Sighing, Joe began washing glasses from last night, grateful that the pub was currently quiet. He was starting to wonder if he'd made a mistake not admitting who he was to Angela. At least that way he wouldn't now be running around in circles like a headless chicken, and presumably Birdie's daughter wouldn't have suspected him of being a closet assassin. She might even have confided in him.

And now, the sudden appearance of Angela's uncle just muddied the waters even further. He didn't know what to believe anymore and was becoming more and more convinced that his best course of action would be simply to confront Birdie and ask her. Slamming the tea towel down, Joe made up his mind.

He'd promised the Admiral he'd do nothing but keep an eye on Angela's uncle, but he was done playing Hercule bloody Poirot. As soon as his shift was over, Joe decided he was going to head over to Birdie's house, admit his real identity, and confront her and Angela with his suspicions.

∞∞∞

The Admiral and Jimmy decided to stay in the car overnight so they'd be ready and waiting for the first ferry the next day. After a very satisfying dinner of fish and chips – served in a paper bag just like they used to be – the two men had parked up in the ferry terminal car park and bedded themselves down under a couple of sleeping bags packed by Mabel.

'I'm not sure about the roughing it side of a clandestine operation,' the Admiral grunted, trying to get comfortable without straddling the gear stick. 'Maybe we should give serious consideration to buying a campervan.' Jimmy nodded, while privately thinking there was no way he would entertain the idea of sharing a fifteen foot space ever again with Charles Shackleford unless the fate of the world depended on it.

There was silence for a while, then just when Jimmy was hoping the Admiral had gone off to sleep, the large man spoke again. 'Bit of a rum do, old Norbert having a breakdown like that,' he mumbled, 'Mind you, if I had his bloody name, I'd most likely be two steps away from the funny farm.'

'Well, looking at his house, I'd guess his problems are more about money,' speculated Jimmy while trying to avoid the seat belt buckle inching its way up his nether regions, 'He obviously never won insurance salesman of the year. Still, he's obviously on the mend or he wouldn't have turned up in Dartmouth would he?'

'Who knows,' muttered the Admiral with a frown, 'Could be he has suspicions of his own about his brother's widow…'

They arrived on the Isle of Wight bright and early the next morning - well, the weather was bright, the Admiral and Jimmy were sporting various aches and pains ranging from a stiff neck to a possible hernia They didn't smell too sweet either.

'That's what a night in a damn car does for you,' commented the Admiral as they drove off the ferry. 'We're definitely investing in a camper van Jimmy lad,' he added, ignoring the small man's less than enthusiastic silence.

The ferry dropped them off in Fishbourne on the north of the island. From there it was a short drive to Bembridge where Michael Wellington's old hotel was situated.

The Whitecliffe was an imposing Victorian building described by the guide book as *luxury boutique*

'That means you have to take out a bloody mortgage to stay in a room you can't swing a cat in,' commented the Admiral as they climbed stiffly out of the car.

'Nevertheless Sir, it's the best place for us to stay if we're looking to find out about Michael Wellington,' Jimmy commented before heading determinedly up the steps to the ornate front door.

It was obvious a lot of money had been spent on the interior and the small man paused, whistling slightly as he took in the sweeping mahogany staircase and the huge ornate marble fireplace which dominated the hall. Everything gleamed and he couldn't help but hesitate before stepping onto the beautiful tiled floor. He wondered whether Michael had been responsible for the décor or whether it had been done since his death. Either way, it must have been sold for a pretty packet.

'Can I help you?'

With a start Jimmy became aware of a large, politely smiling woman sitting at a mahogany desk halfway down the hall. Just as he was about to respond, the Admiral breezed in saying, 'Bloody hell, I bet there are a few yuppies staying in this place.'

The woman's smile became a little strained, so Jimmy hastily stepped forward and determinedly asked if they had *two single rooms* available for one night. The woman looked down at her book and after a couple of seconds nodded her head.

'How much?' the Admiral asked brusquely. When she primly quoted the price, Jimmy winced as Charles Shackleford commented loudly, 'I want to stay the night, not buy the bollocking place.'

Her smile became so fixed, Jimmy suspected she'd get lock jaw if she kept it up much longer. Frowning over at the Admiral, he said quickly, 'That will be fine, thank you. Would you like us to pay in advance?'

'Birdie must be worth a fortune,' muttered the Admiral when they reconvened an hour later. 'She has to have sold this place for at least a couple of million.'

'But if you believe the rumours,' Jimmy added drily, 'Old Barney was doing his level best to put a bloody great dent in her nest egg.'

'And that's a damn good motive for murder Jimmy lad,' the Admiral commented sagely before glancing back towards the imposing front door and continuing, 'I don't think questioning old frosty features in there is going to get us anywhere. She looks like she's been sucking on a bloody lemon.'

'It might be a good idea to let her calm down a bit,' agreed Jimmy shaking his head. 'Why don't we head over to the sailing club Marcus and Michael belonged to – see if we get any joy there?'

'Sounds like a plan Jimmy, and if we play our cards right, they'll let us use the facilities. I could eat a scabby donkey between two mattresses right about now. I think I've got my Royal Dart Yacht Club membership somewhere,' he added, rummaging around in the inside pocket of his jacket.

Jimmy frowned, 'When was the last time you did any yachting Sir?'

'What's that got to do with anything?' the Admiral grunted, finally holding up a crumpled card triumphantly. 'They serve a decent pint at half the price. Always good to know if the Ship's closed.'

Bembridge sailing club sported a delightful dining room and bar with lots of painted wood and pictures of boats – all very New England. There was also a charming covered veranda, perfectly positioned to watch the world sail by.

As the Admiral had predicted, they were welcomed with open arms and half an hour later were cosily ensconced on the veranda with a pint each and a packet of pork scratchings.

'I think Emily would like it here,' mused Jimmy taking an appreciative sip of his beer. The only sounds were the ever present cries of the seagulls fighting over scraps and the clank clank of the yachts moored up in front of them as their rigging moved in the slight breeze. For once the Admiral didn't break the peace and quiet, and simply nodded his head, content to watch a group of dinghies sailing in the distance.

'CHARLIE SHACKLEFORD AS I LIVE AND BLOODY BREATHE.'

Suddenly the peace was shattered and the two men turned as one to observe the owner of the booming voice. For a second the Admiral frowned, then suddenly his expression cleared and he got to his feet shouting, 'Daisy bollocking May, I can't believe it. What the bloody hell are you doing here?'

'Me and the missus came here when I retired - nigh on ten years ago now.' The large man grinned.

'You've been out for ten years?' The Admiral shook his head, 'Bloody hell, how long's it been since we last had a run ashore together?'

'Must be twenty years give or take, and you're still as bloody ugly as a bag of spanners.'

The two men clasped hands, laughing delightedly before the Admiral turned to Jimmy. 'Daisy was a WAFU, and as you can clearly see, it wasn't me who was hit with the ugly stick.'

'Who you calling Wet And Flipping Useless?' Daisy responded, clapping the Admiral on the back. 'I'll have you know I was a well respected, long standing member of the Fleet Air Arm.'

'I'll say,' the Admiral chuckled, 'You were learning to fly when Pontius was the senior bloody Pilot.

'Daisy, this is Jimmy Noon, the best Master At Arms I ever had.'

Jimmy reddened at the unexpected praise and took the newcomer's hand. 'Pleased to meet you Sir,' he said respectfully.

'None of your bloody bowing and scraping young Noon, we're not in the Navy now, although some of us tend to forget it.' He turned back to the Admiral. 'What are you drinking both of you, we've got a lot of catching up to do.'

Twenty minutes later the three of them were on their third pint and tucking into a delicious lamb and mint pie and mash.

'So what brings you to Dinosaur Island Charlie?' Daisy asked as they finally sat back, stuffed fit to bursting.

'To tell you the truth Daisy, we're after a bit of Intel. Chap by the name of Marcus Tennant. Took a tumble off his yacht somewhere near here about seven years ago now.'

Daisy frowned and nodded thoughtfully. 'I remember old Marcus. Knew him quite well in fact. Bloody rum do what happened. I told him racing in the bloody Cowes Regatta was no place for a youngen.'

'Was his daughter on board when he died then?' the Admiral asked sharply.

'That she was Charlie. And old Marcus died trying to save her...'

CHAPTER 11

'I thought no-one knew what had happened,' Jimmy commented.

'Well, as far as the actual sequence of events, that's true,' Daisy answered with a shrug. 'But when the yacht came back in, the daughter was screaming about leaving her dad to die, and she was wet right down to her birthday suit.'

'Could she have dived in or something, you know, trying to save her father?' the Admiral asked.

'Possibly, if she could swim,' Daisy answered bluntly. 'But the girl couldn't even do a few strokes. She was hysterical when they got her off the boat. It was up to Michael to explain what had happened.'

'Do you mean Michael Wellington?' questioned Jimmy.

'Aye, that's him. Used to own that huge pile of bricks up on the hill,' Daisy responded, waving his hand vaguely towards the Whitecliffe Hotel. 'He was crewing for Marcus. There were only the three of them on board that day. Someone called Jamie was supposed to be the third crew member but he went down with some kind of food poisoning, so - Angela, I think her name was – begged her father to let her stand in.' Daisy shook his head.

'I don't know what Marcus was bloody thinking. I know she went out on the boat with him regularly for fun, and I suppose he thought no harm could come to her as long as she was wearing her life jacket.' He sighed. 'Racing's a different ball game. Dangerous to anyone without experience. There were loads of experienced sailors hanging around willing to crew for anyone who'd have them, but no, Marcus decided to take his daughter along – and it cost him his life.'

'So what did Michael say actually happened?' Jimmy asked breathlessly.

Daisy took a sip of his pint before answering. 'Apparently they were retiring from the race - I think Marcus got hit by something. He was sitting in the cockpit removing his life jacket to have a look at his shoulder, when Angela supposedly went overboard. He didn't wait to put his jacket back on, but dove in to save her.

'Marcus managed to get his daughter back onto the boat, but then according to Angela, his shoulder seized up and he just sank.'

'Where was Michael when all this was happening and why didn't he have a go at trying to save Marcus himself?' questioned the Admiral, wondering if he already knew the answer.

Daisy sighed. 'Michael said that by the time he came topside, Marcus had already disappeared, but he didn't dare leave Angela alone on the yacht to dive in and look for him. Apparently she was out of control even then. Instead Michael called the coast guard then stayed put for about half an hour trying to spot Marcus in the water.

'Problem was, the stupid fool had taken his life jacket off.' Daisy shook his head again. 'A complete bloody no no, not for any reason. Even the most inexperienced sailors know that for God's sake. I can't imagine what Marcus was thinking.'

There was a short silence as the three of them pictured what had happened on The Tempest seven years ago.

'Another pint?' Daisy asked eventually.

'Let me,' Jimmy volunteered, getting up and quickly heading towards the bar.

'Did you know that Michael was having an affair with Marcus's wife Birdie?' asked the Admiral carefully after a couple of minutes.

Daisy looked briefly surprised, then nodded. 'Everyone knew,' he said simply.

'But he still let his wife's bit on the side crew for him?' the Admiral questioned sceptically

Daisy shrugged. 'They'd been close friends since school, and it was common knowledge that Marcus batted for the other side.'

'Marcus was a harry hoofter?' the Admiral questioned incredulously, glancing over at Jimmy as the small man returned with their drinks.

Daisy nodded. 'I think he was quite content for Michael to keep his wife happy between the sheets. Better his best friend than his brother Norbert.'

'What do you mean?' asked Jimmy sitting back down.

Daisy took a long swallow of his beer before speaking. 'It was well before we moved here, but apparently Birdie went out with Norbert before Marcus. It seems that everyone thought they'd make a match of it at the time, but from what I can gather, at the end of the day, it was Marcus who had the dosh, being an up and coming corporate lawyer, even if he did swim for the other team.'

Daisy shook his head again, this time sadly. 'Norbert hung around after Marcus died, right up until Birdie married Michael, then he left and never came back.' Daisy took another swallow of his pint. 'Maybe if he'd stayed a bit longer, he'd have got lucky because poor old

Michael popped his clogs a couple of years later – in your neck of the woods I think it was.'

'That's right,' the Admiral agreed, 'Fell off a battlement at Berry Pomeroy castle near Totnes.'

Daisy winced and pulled a face. 'Well Birdie didn't linger after Michael had his first and last flying lesson. Once the funeral was over, she sold up lock stock and barrel and left along with Angela. No idea where she went then.'

'Dartmouth,' supplied the Admiral grimly. 'She went to Dartmouth and married an old oppo of mine – Barney Bennett.'

Daisy raised his eyebrows. 'Blimey, husband number three, she certainly gets through them.'

'And now there could be a number four,' Jimmy added distastefully. 'Barney Bennett died a few weeks ago in a supposed car accident.'

'But you don't think it was an accident,' responded Daisy reading between the lines. 'Does that mean you don't think the other two deaths were accidental either?'

'Spot on Daisy,' the Admiral said, 'But so far we haven't been able to prove anything.'

Daisy stared thoughtfully at them both before heaving a big sigh. 'Well if we're going to be putting our thinking caps on gentlemen, we're going to need another pint on standby…'

'So, what makes you think Marcus and Michael's deaths weren't down to the winds of bloody fate?' Daisy was beginning to slur his words slightly and all three were now pretty well oiled.

The Admiral frowned. 'Well, for one thing, burying three bollocking husbands without one of them dying of old age has to be a bit suspect, and we had a visit from Michael Wellington's son. Did you know he had one?'

Daisy nodded. 'Michael didn't say much about him and I never saw the boy visit. Got the feeling things hadn't ended up on the rosy side between Michael and the lad's mother. Mind you, I suppose he's not really a lad anymore. What did he want with you?'

'He reckoned his father was murdered for threatening to go to the plod about something Birdie did. Apparently Michael left a letter for Joe – that's his son - telling him he was tired of keeping whatever it was a secret.'

'So this Joe thought old Birdie had put an end to his dad to stop him from spilling the beans about something bad?' Jimmy and the Admiral nodded simultaneously.

'Bit bloody farfetched,' Daisy commented taking a sip of his pint. 'I mean Birdie wasn't even on the Tempest when Marcus went to visit Davy Jones' locker.' He paused thoughtfully, then added, 'I suppose Birdie might have put Michael up to getting rid of her husband. That could be what he was talking about in that letter to his son. But why? It wasn't like Marcus was bothered Michael was bonking his missus.'

'But Angela might have been if she'd found out about the affair,' offered Jimmy sombrely. 'Whatever relationship Angela had with her mother then, we've been told there's no love lost between them now.'

'Joe reckons he came down to Dartmouth to do a bit of snooping and got to know her at the pub. She might have been shamming, but according to Joe, Angela actually offered to pay him to do her mother in.'

Daisy whistled. 'Bloody hell, have you been to the police?' Jimmy shook his head.

'It's only his word against hers, and whatever their private feelings about each other, the act they put on for everyone else is all warm and touchy bloody feely.'

'And now Norbert's turned up in Dartmouth,' added the Admiral, 'It might be because he fancies having another crack at Birdie now she's buried husband number three. But if I were him, I'd be a bit bloody hesitant about tying the knot given her track record.'

'And by all accounts, Norbert wasn't a happy bunny when Birdie started sharing her favours with Michael instead of him,' volunteered Jimmy, shaking his head.

'No, you're right about that,' Daisy said with a sigh. He glanced around as the evening crowd began to drift in, and leaned forward conspiratorially. 'I'm not one for muck spreading, and what I'm about to tell you might be a load of old bollocks, but the dates fit.

'The fact is, rumour had it that Angela wasn't really Marcus's daughter at all - she was Norbert's.'

CHAPTER 12

Mabel's transformation was nothing short of miraculous. What Birdie Bennett had achieved in one short day knocked twenty years off her, and murderer or no murderer, Emily had promptly booked herself in for the following morning.

As it turned out, she was effectively killing two birds with one stone as the first person she spoke to on entering the salon was Birdie's daughter Angela, who apparently worked alongside her mother.

She couldn't help but think that Joe's assessment of the young woman was a bit harsh as Angela took her coat and explained that her mother had been held up but would be at the salon in the next twenty minutes. The young girl was both pleasant and polite, smilingly making Emily a cup of tea and chatting about the merits of various treatments.

Not wanting to waste an interrogation opportunity, Emily sipped her tea and murmured how sorry she was to hear of her stepfather's passing.

'Thank you,' Angela responded with a small grimace. 'It's very sad and certainly knocked my mother for six. She and Barney were very much in love.'

'It's certainly sad for your mother,' Emily continued sympathetically, 'To lose three husbands in such tragic circumstances.'

Angela looked over at her sharply and all of a sudden, Emily could see why Joe Wellington disliked her. There was something cold about her eyes. And not just cold, but calculating.

'I wasn't aware my mother's previous marriages were common knowledge,' Angela said carefully, folding up some clean towels.

'Well you know how people are,' Emily responded quickly, her heart abruptly beating faster, 'And Birdie has a lot of good friends in Dartmouth.'

'Certainly inquisitive ones,' the young woman countered brusquely. She picked up the towels, and muttering, 'If you'll excuse me,' she took them into the back room and shut the door.

Feeling increasingly uncomfortable, Emily finished her tea and glanced down at her watch. Birdie was now half an hour late. She really didn't know what to do. Putting her cup down, she was about to get up when the telephone rang. Opening the door abruptly, Angela hurried over to the desk to answer it. Reasoning that she had a valid excuse (and let's be honest, how often does *that* happen), Emily did her best to eavesdrop while looking nonchalantly down at her magazine, but at the end of the day all she got were a few words offered in heated whispers.

After a couple of minutes, Birdie's daughter abruptly slammed down the phone before saying brusquely, 'I'm afraid my mother is not coming into the salon today Mrs. Noon, you'll have to make another appointment.'

'Oh, that's a shame,' replied Emily, genuinely disappointed that she wasn't about to undergo the same transformation as Mabel. 'I hope everything's alright?'

She stared expectantly at Angela, but Birdie's daughter simply smiled tightly and said, 'I'm afraid my mother's double booked herself.' Then, giving Emily her coat back, she opened the door and waited until the elderly matron reluctantly walked through it. As the door closed behind her, Emily heard Angela hang up the Closed sign.

Uncertain what to do next, Emily decided to loiter for a bit, and for the next ten minutes she stood over the road and observed Birdie's Groom Room. She could see Angela through the window on the phone again and couldn't help but notice that her gestures were getting increasingly agitated.

At length Birdie's daughter slammed down the phone and sat down on the stool behind the counter, biting her fingernail and staring out of the window in obvious anxiety.

After another five minutes she finally stood up, grabbed her coat and hurried out of the shop. Emily stood indecisively for a few seconds, wondering if she should follow, but as she was making up her mind, Angela headed over to a car parked about fifty yards away, climbed in and drove off.

∞∞∞∞

'Blimey Sir, I can't say I'm feeling quite the ticket this morning,' Jimmy groaned, eying the fried breakfast in front of him queasily.

'No bloody stamina Jimmy lad,' the Admiral commented tucking into his own breakfast with a gusto. 'You'd have slept like a baby if you'd had a few tots of rum to finish with.'

Jimmy frowned, picking listlessly at his bacon. 'It's a good job I didn't Sir,' he remarked tartly, 'Somebody had to get you back to the hotel. What would I have told Mabel had you fallen in the bloody sea and drowned like old Marcus? As it was, I had all on to stop you from going skinny dipping. That poor woman, innocently out to get herself some fish and chips, nearly had a coronary as it was, thinking you were about to do yourself in. If you'd taken it into your head to drop your trousers, you'd probably have finished her off.'

'Bloody good shindig though,' the Admiral commented unrepentantly, waving his fork towards his disgruntled friend, 'Had 'em hanging off my every word.'

'With respect Sir, most of what you were telling them was a complete load of bollocks,' Jimmy responded irritably. 'Your account of your time in Borneo sounded almost word for word like the plot of the *Bridge Over The River Kwai.*'

'Never let the truth get in the way of a good dit,' the Admiral responded cheerfully. 'Now then, what time are we aiming to get off? I think we've found out everything we're likely to about old Marcus's impromptu swim, and if we get a move on, we might manage to catch an early ferry.'

∞∞∞

'So, Angela said Birdie had doubled book herself?' asked Jimmy dubiously, 'I wonder what she meant by that?'

Emily nodded. 'I tried to find out, but she just hustled me out of the salon as quickly as possible. The only words I heard were, 'Too soon,' and, 'Not ready.' I got the feeling that whatever Birdie was doing, her daughter wasn't very happy about it.'

Jimmy frowned and shook his head. He and the Admiral had only been back at the Admiralty for a little over an hour after stopping off for a swift half at the Ship.

Mabel leaned forward excitedly. 'I was speaking to Agnes at the WI this morning,' she breathed conspiratorially, 'And she said she'd heard that Birdie had run off with someone. Maybe that's what Angela was talking about.'

'Could be Marcus's brother – the one with the dodgy name in the Floating Bridge,' added Emily, 'Seems a bit suspect that this should happen just after he pops up.'

Jimmy agreed, 'Especially after what we discovered back at Marcus's old sailing club.' He turned to the Admiral who had so far been uncharacteristically silent. 'Would you like to tell them about our findings Sir?'

Unfortunately the Admiral wasn't in any position to take part in the conversation. Mabel's transformation into Dartmouth's answer to *Joan Collins* had rendered him unable to string two words together – a phenomenon previously unheard of.

After a loud cough failed to bring him back down to earth, Jimmy sighed and quickly recounted the details of their discoveries on the Isle of Wight.

'So, Angela could be Norbert's daughter,' Emily whispered shaking her head. 'Do you think Angela knows it?'

Jimmy shrugged. 'It would explain any anger issues she has with her mother, but whether she suspects or not, I still can't imagine Birdie doing a runner with Norbert or anybody else without running it past her.'

Jimmy looked over at the Admiral again with a frown before saying loudly, 'I think we could do with a glass of Port to help the old grey matter. What do you think Sir?'

The mention of Port was more effective in bringing Charles Shackleford out of his trance. The Admiral nodded and, after giving one last incredulous glance in Mabel's direction, he asked if anyone had heard from Joe Wellington.

The two ladies shook their heads, and the Admiral suggested that Jimmy do the honours while he searched out Joe's number and gave Michael Wellington's son a quick call.

Five minutes later he returned to the study, his face grave. 'Number's not recognized,' he said, shaking his head. 'It seems our young friend wasn't quite on the up and up with us. I called the Floaters, and they told me he'd missed his shift this lunchtime and they had no idea where he was.'

He took the proffered glass of Port from Jimmy and took a grateful sip. 'I smell a big bloody rodent ladies and gentlemen. It can't be coincidence that Birdie goes AWOL and then Joe.' He paused, sighing worriedly as Jimmy put his concerns into words.

'I hope Michael's son hasn't decided to take matters into his own hands…'

CHAPTER 13

'Do we know where Joe's digs are?' asked the Admiral.

'Didn't he say he was staying on a boat?' offered Emily with a frown.

'That's right,' Mabel added eagerly, 'He said he was staying on Ben Shepherd's yacht – you know, Tory's friend.'

'Right then,' the Admiral responded decisively, 'I'll give Victory a ring and get Ben's number, then we'll ask him if we can have a bit of a shufti round his boat, see if Joe's left any clues as to where he's buggered off to.'

Half an hour later they were on the higher ferry, crammed into Jimmy's little Fiat. 'We've got about forty five minutes before Ben meets us at the boat float,' Jimmy confirmed with the Admiral, 'Do you think we should make a quick stop at the Floating Bridge Sir? See if anyone might know where Joe could have got to?'

Charles Shackleford nodded his head. 'Good plan Jimmy lad. We can have a swift half while we're waiting.'

'That's two swift halves you'll have had today by my reckoning,' commented Emily tartly from the back, 'Not to mention that large glass of Port you had not an hour ago. I think you'll be having half a shandy Jim.'

Jimmy winced at his wife's resolute tone and the Admiral muttered something about Port being medicinal under his breath, but neither man argued, and a few minutes later they were entering the dim interior of the Floating Bridge.

'Let's sit up at the bar,' Mabel suggested boldly, still firmly in *Joan Collin's* mode. 'It will be easier to ask questions.'

As it turned out, the bar stools were quite high and Mabel didn't appear to have quite the same dexterity as the Hollywood star. 'You'll have to give me a hand Charlie,' the matron conceded after almost taking out the barman's eye with her handbag as she inadvertently let go of the handle on her third attempt.

With a sigh, the Admiral stepped forward, and placing his hand under Mabel's ample posterior, he heaved upwards. Unfortunately he slightly misjudged the height of the stool and only the beer taps lined up in front prevented her from going head first over the bar. As it was, she head butted the Bay's Ale pump and landed back on the stool with a loud, 'Woomph.'

Cringing, the Admiral hurriedly murmured his apologies and put a conciliatory arm around his beloved. As he mumbled, 'There, there,' he decided it was probably best not to mention the large B imprinted across her forehead in the forlorn hope that it might have gone down by the time they got home.

After giving Emily a pleading glance, he coughed and asked the two ladies what they wanted to drink.

'I think we'll have a Prows Echo. What do you say Mabel?' Emily stated boldly, defying the Admiral to argue.

Sighing, the Admiral replaced the ten-pound note in his hand with a twenty and patted Mabel's shoulder awkwardly, saying, 'Only the best for my little dove.' Fortunately for him, Mabel was still slightly dazed, or she'd have spotted a rat immediately in his saccharine coated words.

'We were expecting to see Joe here today,' the large man murmured casually as he paid for their drinks.

'Don't you mean Tony, Sir?' Jimmy asked, giving the Admiral a swift kick in the shin. 'Ow… err… yes, Tony. Nice chap. Isn't he in today?'

The barman eyed them both narrowly, then shrugged. 'He should have been here at eleven, but he didn't turn up for his shift.'

'Didn't he call or anything?' asked Jimmy in his best disinterested voice.

'He's only seasonal,' was the equally lacklustre response, 'They come and go – but very rarely give us much warning when they decide to up sticks.

'Are you friends of Tony?' he asked with a little more interest, 'If you are and you see the lazy good for nothing, tell him he owes us fifty quid, 'cos he was paid 'til the end of the bloody week.'

'When did he come in last?' Jimmy asked ignoring the barman's gripe.

'Last night. He did the late shift,' came the irritated reply. 'He said he'd be here this morning, but as you can see…'

'Did he leave on his own?' asked Jimmy with a frown.

'I've no idea' the barman answered impatiently, 'I don't keep tabs on employee's social habits. Now if you'll excuse me, I have work to do.'

The Admiral scowled as the barman went to serve other customers. 'It's all looking pretty bloody suspect to me. We've got Joe and Birdie, both off God knows where. I've got this feeling if we find one of them, we'll find the other. I just hope neither of them are juggling halos when we do.'

They didn't have to wait at the boat float on Dartmouth River front for very long before they spotted Ben Shepherd's dinghy motoring towards them. Before boarding, the Admiral glanced at his watch. It was nearly four thirty. His gut told him that time was running out, but for who, he couldn't say. He just felt the same sense of urgency in his bladder that usually resulted in a visit to the heads.

Mabel had decided to abstain from clambering around a small yacht moored in the middle of the river on account of the fact that her sea legs weren't quite as good as Joan Collins – not having attended quite so many cocktail parties aboard floating gin palaces.

Emily, despite being next in line as president of Ladies Afloat and with excellent sea legs, kindly offered to remain on the jetty to keep her company. Their decision might also have had something to do with the warm late afternoon sunshine and the prospect of a crafty ninety-nine.

While Ben was mooring up, the Admiral solicitously helped Mabel sit down onto an empty bench. He took extra care with the elderly matron, hoping it might give him a few extra points when she got home and noticed the tattoo on her forehead which unfortunately didn't appear to be going down any.

Two minutes later he and Jimmy were clambering onto the dinghy and struggling into their life jackets. As they eased away from the jetty, the Admiral asked Tory's friend when he'd last seen Tony.

'Don't you mean Joe?' asked Ben confused.

'Bloody hell,' the Admiral grumbled, 'Our Mr. Wellington wouldn't make much of a private eye would he? No good being under cover if you can't remember what your bollocking name's supposed to be.'

Steering the dinghy towards his yacht, Ben confirmed that he'd last seen Joe that morning. 'He'd told me he was working at the Floaters all day, so I asked if he'd mind me doing some work on the boat while it was empty. But when I arrived, he was still here. Said he was waiting for a water taxi.'

'About what time was that?' interrupted Jimmy.

Ben raised his eyebrows, thinking. 'I would say just after twelve.'

'Did he say where he was going?' asked Jimmy apprehensively.

Ben shook his head. 'I didn't ask. I just thought he was a bit late for his shift at the pub.'

'Did he seem anxious in any way?' enquired the Admiral.

'Now you come to mention it, he did seem a bit out of sorts. He wasn't here long. As soon as the water taxi arrived, he went below and came back up with a large rucksack a minute or so later.'

'I don't suppose you saw what was in the rucksack,' the Admiral commented hopefully.

Ben shook his head. 'But whatever it was, it was heavy. When he threw it down into the taxi it made a right thunk. In fact the skipper laughingly asked him if he'd got a body in there.'

Chuckling, Ben turned towards the approaching yacht so didn't notice that neither Jimmy nor the Admiral were laughing.

'I'm not sure we'll find anything here to tell us where Joe's gone Sir,' Jimmy commented in a low voice. 'I just get this feeling that we're wasting time we haven't got.' The Admiral nodded, not surprised that Jimmy was feeling the same sense of urgency.

'Well, we're here now,' was all the large man said, 'We might as well give it a quick once over. If we can't find out where Joe's gone, we're up the creek without a bloody paddle Jimmy lad – and that's without the added question of where Angela fits in this cake and arse party.'

A couple of minutes later they were climbing the short ladder into Dartmouth Belle's cockpit. Ben unlocked the door leading down into the cabin and waved them inside.

The Admiral went down first, clambering down the steep stairs carefully to let his eyes get used to the gloom. Once at the bottom he stepped sideways into the small galley to avoid receiving an impromptu nose job from Jimmy following closely behind him. The two men looked round, noting the dishes in the sink and the clothes lying around the cabin.

'Well, if he's done a runner, it certainly wasn't planned,' observed Jimmy, stepping cautiously to avoid the garments littering the floor.

'It's almost like he was panicking about something,' the Admiral mused, glancing round at the cupboard doors left open.

Jimmy shook his head in frustration. 'There doesn't look to be anything here to tell us where he's gone though.'

'What's that?' the Admiral asked, pointing to a small card on the floor under the table. Jimmy crouched down to pick it up, holding it up to the light as he got to his feet. On the front was a drawing of a ruined castle with words *Castle Café* printed in neat lettering underneath. The words were underlined in biro along with the letter B and the number five scrawled underneath. Turning the card over, both men drew in their breath almost simultaneously. There was a simple map giving directions to Berry Pomeroy Castle.

The same castle from whose walls Michael Wellington plunged to his death five years ago...

CHAPTER 14

An hour later they were impatiently waiting for the car ferry to take them back to the Admiralty.

'It stands to reason that the B on the card is short for Birdie,' the Admiral commented, 'And the number five could well be a time.' He shook his head, adding anxiously, 'What the bloody hell is the boy doing? Why would he want to meet with Birdie at the place his dad snuffed it? Damn creepy if you ask me.'

'He did seem pretty convinced that Birdie was responsible for his father's death,' observed Jimmy. 'It's not beyond the realms of possibility that he's decided to bypass the plod.'

'I really can't see why Mabel and I can't come with you,' said Emily petulantly.

Jimmy sighed and swivelled round to look at his irate wife. 'It's getting late,' he offered patiently, 'You've been to Berry Pomeroy Castle before love – it's a pile of ruins surrounded by trees. By the time we get there, the valley will be completely in shadow, making the ground doubly treacherous.'

'Not to mention the fact that we have no bloody idea what we're likely to find,' added the Admiral.

Jimmy nodded and reached out a hand to Emily. 'We need you and Mabel to be on the end of the phone,' he said earnestly, 'Just in case we need help quickly.'

'Why don't you just call the police?' Mabel asked worriedly, 'I mean, if Birdie's not turned up, they might be looking for her by now.'

'And tell them what?' the Admiral scoffed. 'The whole cake and arse party sounds like complete bollocks, even to us. We've got nothing but a bunch of might haves and maybes, and a card advertising Berry Pomeroy Castle. The plod are going to think we've lost the damn plot.'

'All we intend to do is check it out,' continued Jimmy soothingly, 'I promise we won't do anything foolish. The place will probably be deserted anyway.'

'And we'll take Pickles with us,' interjected the Admiral as Jimmy twisted back round to drive onto the ferry, 'You know how good Springers are at flushing out game. If there's any funny business going on, he'll let us know about it.'

Mabel privately thought it was more likely they wouldn't see Pickles for dust if he happened to get the scent of a rabbit, but she refrained from mentioning it. Instead she glanced over at Emily who was already looking back at her knowingly, and murmured, 'We'll give them a half an hour head start.' Emily nodded without answering.

It was getting on for eight pm and the shadows were most definitely lengthening by the time the two men arrived at the gate to the Castle grounds.

'Do you think we should leave the car here Sir?' asked Jimmy peering dubiously through the windscreen into the tree shrouded gloom in front of them.

Now they were here, both men felt reluctant to vacate the relative safety of the car. The only passenger showing any enthusiasm for an evening hike in spooky surroundings was Pickles, who was now busy panting and drooling excitedly over their shoulders.

After dithering for a minute or so, the Admiral heaved a sigh. 'Come on Jimmy lad, it's no good sitting here and waiting for trouble to come to us. It's time to finish this business once and for all. We owe it to Barney Bennett if nobody else. Let's get Operation *Murderous Marriages* over and done with.'

With that, he climbed out of the car and went to open the back door before Pickles decided to use Jimmy's head as a springboard. Clipping on the Spaniel's leash, he went round to the boot where they'd stashed a length of rope, a couple of torches and some makeshift weapons.

A few seconds later, Jimmy joined him and they eyed their homemade arsenal doubtfully. What had seemed ridiculously excessive back at the Admiralty, felt pathetic now they were surrounded by menacing shadowy silence.

Coughing to cover up his unease, the Admiral reached inside and grabbed hold of the rope, looping it round his middle until it was secure. Then he put one of the torches into his pocket before taking hold of an old walking stick he'd found in the garage.

Swishing it around in his best gentleman spy manner, he accidentally smacked the stick against the back of Jimmy's legs. The small man went down with an audible grunt and only narrowly avoided head butting the bumper.

Ignoring his friend's moans, the Admiral nodded satisfactorily at his weapon's effectiveness, and went back in to grab a can of home-made pepper spray which had been languishing in the cupboard since he'd made it for Victory on the occasion of her first date.

Tucking it into his pocket, he finally looked down at his groaning companion. 'Come on Jimmy lad,' he whispered loudly, 'Rolling around on the ground's not going to help anything. We're here to do a job and by God, we're going to do it.'

Jimmy looked up at the Admiral incredulously. 'You nearly took my legs off at the knees Sir,' he hissed furiously, grasping hold of the open boot in an effort to leaver himself up.

The Admiral frowned, then shook his head sympathetically. 'I understand you dragging your feet Jimmy boy,' he said benevolently, 'But putting it off won't make it all go away.'

'Thanks for your help... Sir,' Jimmy panted sarcastically, finally pulling himself back onto his feet.

'You're welcome,' responded the Admiral solemnly, going back to stabbing the air with his do-it-yourself javelin, fortunately this time in the opposite direction.

Shaking his head, Jimmy leaned into the boot. He was seriously beginning to doubt the wisdom of their actions, however heroic. But for good or ill, they were here now, and, if nothing else, it was about time they finally found out what the bloody hell was going on.

He put the second torch into his pocket, then pulling out an old rounders bat and an unused can of *Old Spice* the Admiral had apparently had for Christmas twenty years ago, he shut the boot as quietly as he could.

Then, hobbling determinedly towards his former commanding officer, he murmured quietly, 'Lead on Sir.'

After five minutes of walking, they spied a track leading away from the road and down through the trees. After a slight hesitation, the Admiral glanced back to see if Jimmy objected, then left the road and followed the trail. Luckily the ground was only slightly damp and the downward slope made it reasonably easy going. Nevertheless they were panting slightly before the path came to an end next to a small wooden building – probably the Castle Café advertised on the card they'd found.

The two men barely noticed the small tea rooms however, as all their attention was taken up by the ghostly ruins that rose up in front of them. Wordlessly they stood and stared at the castle gate house and wall, still almost completely intact, before moving on to the decaying mansion housed inside. With the light slowly disappearing, the empty windows were dark and gaping. Pickles, previously so eager and excited, whined softly and shivered.

'Isn't this castle supposed to be one of the most haunted in Britain?' asked the Admiral in a low voice.

Jimmy didn't answer. Instead he turned back towards the road they'd strayed from earlier and followed it with his eyes to its culmination - a large open area about a hundred yards away. 'There's the car park,' he murmured squinting into the gloom. 'There look to be at least two cars in it. Do you recognize either of them Sir?'

The Admiral shook his head. 'I can barely tell what bloody colour they are let alone the make,' he grumbled. 'Shall we go and have a quick shufti? It might help if we get the registration numbers.'

Jimmy nodded. 'But before we go, let's just check the gate's locked. If it is, we're going to have to find another way in.'

The two men tiptoed towards the massive gate where the Admiral tried turning the handle. It was locked as they'd suspected and a large padlock reinforced the knowledge that if there was anybody inside, they'd have had difficulty getting in that way. Peering through the bars, Jimmy thought he saw a light flickering through one of the empty windows. Turning to the Admiral, he pointed silently. There it was again. There was definitely someone or something inside the walls.

Quietly, they backed off and hurried towards the car park. Once there, Jimmy made a quick note of the registration numbers. Both cars were pretty muddy and neither was top of the range, but underneath the dirt, the Admiral recognized one of them. It was the car Joe

Wellington had turned up to the Admiralty in on the day he'd asked for their help.

CHAPTER 15

'You're just going to have to be patient Emily,' Mabel said tartly when she stalled the engine for the fourth time. 'I'm not used to driving Charlie's car, so it's going to take me a little time to get my confidence back.'

Emily was saved the necessity of answering as the car jerked forward, seemingly of its own accord, throwing both ladies back into their seats. 'There,' offered Mabel in satisfaction a few minutes later, 'That's better, don't you think Emily?'

They were crawling slowly up the winding road leading away from the River Dart towards the seaside towns nestling in Torbay. Unfortunately, the queue of vehicles recently disembarked from the car ferry and following them up the hill at a snail's pace didn't appear to think it was better at all, and they were passed one after another by a stream of cars containing angry drivers whose actions ranged from raised eyebrows to torrents of abuse. Both ladies kept their eyes firmly on the road. Emily due to acute embarrassment, and Mabel due to acute obliviousness.

At this rate, by the time they reached Berry Pomeroy Castle, any skullduggery was likely to have been afoot and gone home for supper and hot chocolate.

'Mabel dear,' Emily tried as they reached the top of the hill, 'As you say, I am a little more used to driving. Do you think it might be better if I take over?' She glanced over at her friend's mutinous face and played her ace. 'After all, we don't want Charlie or Jimmy to come to a sticky end before we even get there do we?'

Mabel gave Emily a panic-stricken look before swerving to avoid an oncoming tractor. They were so close, the wing mirror came away covered in what looked to be cow dung. A few seconds later they juddered to a halt as Mabel stalled for the fifth time. For a few seconds, neither said anything. Emily due to acute terror, and Mabel due to acute astonishment.

At length, all Emily managed to say through gritted teeth was, 'Give me the keys.' To her credit, Mabel simply handed them over.

∞∞∞

'So how the bloody hell did Joe get in?' asked the Admiral in hushed tones. 'And what about Birdie? Do you think she's inside too?'

'Well, if he met Birdie at five like it said on the card, they would have just walked in through the front gate.' Jimmy indicated Joe's car. 'It looks like the lad's still in there, but I don't know about Birdie. This doesn't look like her car, but to be fair I didn't take much notice when you were breaking into her house. I would have thought she'd have a better motor than this one though with all her dosh. I mean old Barney had a Maserati.'

'Could be the bloody caretaker's for all we know,' the Admiral reasoned, 'But we're not going to find out standing here are we? There's got to be another way in.' He glanced over at the castle, brooding in the approaching dusk, just in time to spot the flickering light again.

'Come on Jimmy lad.' He grabbed the small man's arm, yanked Pickles' leash and hurried all three of them across the grass towards the towering walls, panting, 'There's no time to lose.'

In the end it took them another fifteen minutes to find an opening in the crumbling masonry. Unfortunately, it involved a bit of climbing, a pastime neither man had devoted much time to in the last twenty years.

'Right then,' muttered the Admiral after they'd spent nearly five minutes staring in something approaching panic at the section of wall that had succumbed to nature, if only slightly. 'You follow me up this first bit - we should be able to get up there without much trouble. Then we'll do a recce to find the best way up from there.'

He turned towards Pickles and bent down. 'Right then you sorry excuse for a hound, you're going to have to wait here. I'm trusting you to keep an eye on things, let us know if anything dodgy happens in your section. Do we understand one another?' The Spaniel woofed softly, sorrowfully, looking for all the world as if he knew exactly what his master was saying.

As the Admiral straightened up, Jimmy looked over at him sceptically before turning back to view the almost sheer six-foot-high piece of wall still intact. 'How the hell are we going to climb up that last bit? We're not mountain goats Sir,' he whispered heatedly.

The Admiral didn't answer. Instead, he bent down to roll up his trousers. 'Don't want them getting caught on anything,' he grunted by way of explanation. Then, taking a deep breath, he clambered onto the first large boulder.

Ten minutes later they were standing on the highest portion of the collapsed wall and things were not looking good. Pickles sat watching them five feet below whining softly.

'They couldn't have got in up here,' wheezed Jimmy. 'If Joe's got Birdie inside, there's no bloody way he'd have convinced her to climb up a sheer wall. What earthly reason could he give her that didn't end up with her getting an impromptu face lift like her husband? They must have walked in the normal way.'

There was still enough light left to see the Admiral's answering nod. 'But you'd have thought the English Heritage lot would've checked to see if there were any stragglers before they locked up,' the large man speculated, sitting down on one of the crumbling rocks to get his breath back.

Jimmy shook his head in frustration. 'It doesn't add up. Why would Birdie even consider coming to a spooky pile of old ruins with someone she didn't know? And don't forget she's been off the grid since this morning. She couldn't have been here all that time.' He put his head into his hands, saying in a muffled voice, 'I think we've dropped a bollock this time Sir, I really do.'

The Admiral was about to answer when a light suddenly flashed through one of the gun loops further along the wall.

'Well, someone's in there,' Charles Shackleford muttered, standing up with renewed excitement. 'And whatever it is they're up to, you can bet your Aunty bloody Nellie it's no good.' He turned towards the remaining wall and stared at the brickwork, noting for the first time another narrow window.

'Right then Jimmy lad, here's what we're going to do.' He untied the rope from round his middle, then handed it to Jimmy. 'I want you to climb on my shoulders, then get your foot into that gun loop up there – can you see the hole?' The large man pointed towards the slightly darker patch in the wall and Jimmy nodded, not trusting himself to speak.

'As soon as your foot's secure, I'll give you a boost from this end so you can grab the top of the wall and pull yourself over. Once you're in position, you can secure the rope round one of those merlon whatsits and help me up.'

He stopped triumphantly, then bent forward, waiting for the small man to put his foot into the sling his clasped hands provided. Jimmy stared at his former commanding officer's bowed head feeling a horrible sense of déjà vu. Nothing ever changes, he thought wearily, hoisting the rope over his shoulder and stepping forward.

A couple of seconds later, he was bobbing up and down in midair with his right foot on the Admiral's shoulder and his right hand on the large man's head. His left leg was scrabbling around for the elusive gun loop while his left hand futilely tried to find purchase in the cracks around the bricks. Any minute now he was going to break his bloody neck.

Fortunately, more by luck than judgement, his questing foot finally found the opening it was looking for and he gratefully placed it into the narrow cavity. *Un*fortunately, he was now completely knackered and had no energy to push himself into a position where the Admiral could boost him up to the broken section of the battlement.

He wavered in slow motion with one foot stuck in the gun loop and the Admiral wobbling underneath him like a parody of the Cirque Du Soleil.

'Right Jimmy my boy, it's now or never,' the Admiral grunted.

Ignoring Jimmy's panicked, 'No, wait,' he heaved upwards, luckily giving the small man just enough momentum to push off against the narrow ledge with his left foot. As Jimmy sailed upwards, he managed to grab hold of the parapet which fortunately held his weight. Puffing and panting, he hauled himself towards the top and finally collapsed onto the terrace behind.

'Psst... psst... Come on Jimmy boy, get your bloody arse in gear... What the bollocking hell are you doing – knitting?'

Jimmy was able to tune out the Admiral's whispered demands for all of about two minutes, until his former commanding officer accompanied the last petition with the rounder's bat and walking stick which only narrowly missed his head. Staggering to his feet, Jimmy peered over the broken part of the wall before stepping to the nearest intact section of the battlement. Carefully he tied the rope around the exposed merlon and let the end drop towards the Admiral. He had serious doubts whether his former commanding officer was up to scaling a rampart in semi darkness but was too tired to try and talk him out of it.

A sudden jerk in the rope indicated the Admiral was ready, and bracing himself against the brickwork, Jimmy started tugging. To the small man's complete surprise, a couple of minutes later the Admiral hauled himself up onto the rampart terrace and sank to the ground.

'Right then Jimmy my man,' the Admiral muttered after they'd rested for a few minutes, 'Let's get this bloody operation over with.' He lurched to his feet and looked over the edge to check that Pickles hadn't abandoned his post. After a couple of seconds, he was just able to make out a reassuring wag of the spaniel's tail.

'Which way Sir?' Jimmy whispered as he struggled up wearily.

The Admiral paused for a second, then pointed to the right. Quietly they tiptoed along the wall towards some steps which dropped down to a shadowy opening. 'I think this is St. Margaret's Tower,' whispered the Admiral over his shoulder as he trod carefully down the steps and into the darkness beyond.

'Legend has it old Margaret was locked up in the dungeon at the bottom of this tower by her sister and starved to death.'

Following behind, Jimmy scoffed at the Admiral's gruesome commentary. 'I doubt very much whether Joe would have done something like that to Birdie,' he muttered stepping into the enclosed round space.

'That's where you might be wrong Jimmy lad.'

As his eyes became accustomed to the gloom, Jimmy saw the Admiral standing at the top of a steep flight of stone steps a couple of feet away. His heart beating in trepidation, the small man hurried towards his friend's motionless outline and directed his eyes into the stygian darkness below - where he could just make out the figure of Birdie Bennett sprawled at the bottom, her head twisted to the side. He didn't need to ask whether she was dead.

CHAPTER 16

His Master At Arms training kicking in, Jimmy took out his torch and carefully made his way down to the prone form of Birdie Bennett. Shining the small light over the body, he felt for a pulse which confirmed his worst fears. 'She's definitely dead Sir,' he called softly up to the Admiral, 'By the look of her, I think she might have broken her neck.' Straightening up he added sombrely, 'The body's still warm. I would say she died only minutes ago.'

'The Admiral shook his head and gave a deep sigh. 'We should have got here sooner,' he murmured heavily as Jimmy turned off the torch and rejoined him at the top of the stairs.

'There's nothing we can do for her now,' the small man said sadly. 'We need to call the police Sir. We don't know if her fall was simply a tragic accident or whether she was pushed, but given what we know already, I can't help but suspect this was murder.' Jimmy spoke in whispers, conscious of the possibility that someone was still inside the castle walls. So far they'd heard no-one, but that didn't mean anything.

Quietly the Admiral looked through the narrow aperture casting the meagre light into the tower. It faced towards the car park they'd visited earlier. Both cars could still be seen in the gloom.

Jimmy got out his mobile phone then swore softly. 'There's no signal Sir,' he muttered, 'We need to get to some open ground, see if we can get a reception.'

'I don't think we're on our own Jimmy boy,' the Admiral commented soberly. 'Whoever did this is still hanging around, so we need to hold off using the torches for as long as possible. There's still enough light to see our way if we're careful.'

'So instead of a couple of murderers spotting us from our light, we're more likely to bump into them in the bloody dark.' Jimmy's low voice was sarcastic as he tried to cover his anxiety.

The Admiral gave the small man's shoulder a squeeze. 'Come on Jimmy, there's no sense in hanging around here.' He pointed through the tower opening where another set of steps lead into what was left of the main house. 'If I remember right, we should be able to get back to the courtyard if we cut through there. We're less likely to be seen if we keep to the shadows.'

Taking a deep breath, Jimmy nodded, and as quietly as possible the two men made their way out of the tower and down the steps into the weed choked ruin of what was once a cavernous kitchen.

They stood silently next to what was left of the old fireplace for a few moments to get their bearings in the dim light cast by the skeletal windows high in the moss covered wall. At length, the Admiral pointed towards what had once been the buttery. 'I think we can get through there,' he mouthed stepping away from the safety of the old hearth.

Softly they made their way in the direction the Admiral had indicated, hesitating only briefly before scuttling past a large opening on their right which led to an inner courtyard, open to the evening sky. As they crept round the corner of the buttery, they came out into what a shadowy plaque indicated was the great hall. To their left was the manor's main entrance out into the large courtyard.

'Hopefully we'll be able to get a signal out there,' Jimmy whispered, and was just about to step out into the hall, when a sudden light appeared over an open patch of ground opposite them at the far end of the great hall. Both men froze as they watched the light wax and wane. Someone was obviously shining a torch over the battlement at the edge of the grassy area.

The Admiral pointed, indicating that they should investigate the source of the light. Jimmy shook his head violently and put his hand to his ear mimicking a phone. Charles Shackleford nodded, then gestured for Jimmy to go towards the courtyard before venturing towards the flickering torchlight.

For a couple of seconds, Jimmy stood indecisively, the instinct to follow the Admiral warring with the need to call for help. In the end he sighed in frustration and tiptoed towards the large open space between the ruined mansion and the gatehouse.

The Admiral cautiously made his way towards the flickering light, hugging the wall to keep himself hidden. As he got closer he began to make out voices. Although he couldn't tell what they were saying, the tone was heated and by the time he reached the end of the great hall, it became clear an argument was underway.

Poking his head round the corner, the Admiral drew in his breath sharply. Outlined against the rampart were Angela Bennett and Joe Wellington. Both of them were completely oblivious to his presence as their low voices became more and more heated.

'I told you she'd done it,' spat Angela, pointing a finger into Joe's face, 'That should have been enough, but oh no, you still insisted on *asking* her. Well you heard what she said - she admitted it was all her fault. She *deserved* to die.' She poked Joe in the chest with something and the Admiral realized with horror that she was holding a knife.

'Buggering hell,' he swore to himself softly. He needed to warn Jimmy. He didn't want his former Master At Arms to walk into this bloody cake and arse party. Gripping the edge of the wall, Charles Shackleford slowly, carefully took a step backwards – and promptly trod on the foot of the person standing silently behind him.

He just got chance to utter a small grunt before a hand was quickly slapped over his mouth and what the Admiral felt coldly certain was a gun pressed into his back.

'Don't make a sound,' a low voice whispered into his ear. The Admiral's heart was beating so fast, he wondered if he was about to suffer another heart attack. Somehow he managed to shake his head and the voice continued to whisper in his ear. 'If you think your friend is likely to come and rescue you, then think again. When I last saw him, he was unconscious courtesy of the large rock I hit him with.'

The voice paused, before continuing carelessly, 'At least I think he was unconscious, he could well be dead for all I know. Still, saves having to do it later.'

The ensuing snigger made the Admiral's blood run cold. Whoever the owner of the voice was, there was no compassion at all. The voice was completely empty.

'But we both know she only did it to protect you,' Joe hissed angrily, seemingly oblivious to the knife pointing at his chest. This whole thing is your damn fault Angela. You're the screwed up kid who murdered her father and started this whole bloody chain of events.'

'I don't think it's quite as simple as that Mr. Wellington.' The Admiral was propelled into the light with the gun pressed firmly into the middle of his back as the two protagonists turned in shock.

'Uncle Norbert,' Angela breathed in disbelief. 'What are you doing here? And why is that idiot with you?' The Admiral drew in an indignant breath, but before he had a chance to speak, Norbert Tennant chuckled again and said, 'You're quite right about that my dear, he is a buffoon, and so is his little friend.'

'As for what I'm doing here. Well, I simply wanted to see who your mother's latest squeeze was.' He shook his head in mock distaste before adding, 'Although I have to say I do think she's stooped to an all-time low in going for a date with her late husband's son, even if it was completely unintentional.'

The Admiral stared at Joe, waiting for him to refute Norbert's words, but all Michael Wellington's son did was shake his head miserably, then whisper, 'How did you know?'

Norbert chuckled, a sound that sent shivers up and down the Admiral's spine. 'She came to see me. Spent the entire evening waxing lyrically about her new internet love interest.'

He shook his head, staring intently at the silent Joe. 'I have to say though your online picture isn't a very good likeness,' he commented mockingly. 'Oh, I didn't know her new paramour was *you* exactly. Not until I watched your tender meeting in the car park earlier. All very touching. So sad it wasn't to be a long-term attachment.'

He sighed theatrically. 'I'm only sorry for Birdie's sake that I didn't follow you into St. Margaret's Tower. If I had, the poor love might even now be standing here having a good laugh about the whole thing.'

'How did you find out I was Michael's son?' Joe asked, clearly thrown.

'I knew who you were the moment I saw you in the Floating Bridge,' Norbert responded scathingly. 'You've got your dear father's eyes.'

'Why didn't you say anything,' Joe retorted showing anger again.

'I guessed why you were here,' Norbert answered with a shrug, 'You wanted to find out what had happened to your dear old dad once and for all, so I just sat back and waited to see what you'd do.

'Imagine how surprised I was to find out your strategy was to date both your father's widow *and* his stepdaughter. A little callous, even if you did suspect them both of murder.' He turned to look at Angela who hadn't moved, 'And you seemed to be *so* attached sweetheart, I was loathe to break your heart with the truth.' He chuckled again, 'Although judging by your little spat earlier, you seem to be well acquainted with the facts now.'

'Joe *told* me he was Michael's son,' Angela retorted defensively, 'So, you don't know quite as much as you think you do Uncle Norbert.'

'Oh, that's where you're wrong my dear,' Norbert said smoothly, 'But don't you think you should call me dad?'

Angela stood rooted to the spot, her mouth opening and closing like a fish, blindsided by the abrupt change of subject. The Admiral almost forgot about the gun pressed against his spine as he watched the drama unfolding in front of him.

'Did you think I didn't know you were my daughter?' Norbert asked silkily. 'I knew from the day your mother became pregnant. Of course I offered to do the decent thing, but I couldn't give her nearly as much as Marcus.'

Angela just stood and stared. 'I wanted to confide in you,' she whispered finally, 'But mum wouldn't let me. She said you didn't know.'

'Is that why you pushed my dear brother off his yacht?' Norbert asked neutrally.

Angela stared wildly at him, panting as though she'd run a marathon. 'He didn't care about me,' she cried eventually. 'All he cared about was his bloody boyfriend.'

She stopped and in the torchlight the Admiral could see tears running down her face. 'I didn't mean to kill him. I just wanted us to be together as a family,' she whispered eventually. 'I thought mum would turn to you if Marcus was gone.'

'But instead, she went ahead and married her dead husband's lover,' Norbert spat derisively.

Joe gasped as he got Norbert's meaning. Angela closed her eyes tightly and began to sob, her knife falling to the ground.

'That wasn't supposed to happen,' she murmured brokenly after a while. Norbert stood unmoving, only the Admiral felt the shrug behind him.

'Oh, I'm sure Michael just wanted to do the right thing. After all, he was sleeping with both of them, and I'm sure the guilt was simply crippling.' The voice was back to chilling indifference.

'But once they were married and your mother accidentally let slip that you were my offspring and not his former lover's, clever, clever Michael began to put two and two together. He started to realize that Marcus's death might not have been an accident after all.

'For the longest time he tried to push that day out of his mind, but bit by bit, he began to remember you my dear - screaming and crying, with no *real* explanation of how Marcus had ended up in the water.

'Oh, at first he thought Birdie had put you up to it didn't he? Poor Michael thought you were a victim. But when he finally confronted your mother, she denied knowing anything about it.

'Of course, she couldn't admit to Michael that she'd had her suspicions. She was the only one who knew just how angry you were with Marcus, but at the end of the day she refused to believe a child from her loins capable of murder.' He gave another low chuckle. 'She never realized you were always far more my daughter than hers.'

'But Birdie went ahead and killed my dad anyway,' Joe shouted in despair.

'Is that what she told you?' Norbert asked, not bothering to hide the amusement in his voice. The Admiral felt sick as he began to put the pieces together.

'You killed Michael Wellington. Not Birdie,' Charles Shackleford guessed. He felt the gun tremble as the monster behind him laughed. 'Not such a buffoon after all, Admiral,' he sniggered.

'But she said it was her fau…' Joe started to say.

'I know exactly what she said,' Norbert interrupted stonily. 'She felt responsible you see. She finally understood that her refusal to see what was right in front of her nose had led to your father's death. So, she was absolutely right, it was her fault.' He pushed the Admiral viciously causing him to stumble to the ground before stepping forward, his gun pointing towards the trembling Joe.

'And now dear boy, you've gone and joined our murderous ranks. Very foolish. It *was* you who pushed Birdie down the stairs wasn't it? I can imagine just how angry you felt. I'm sure it hardly took any effort at all – she was such a slight little thing, though perhaps not as slight as she used to be.' He laughed spitefully at his own joke but Joe didn't respond, just stood staring at the ground, shaking his head.

'Of course you've got to join dear old daddy,' Norbert continued matter of factly, 'You *and* the idiot on the floor.' He waved the gun between Joe and the Admiral. 'We can't have the police finding out about the whole sorry mess – not to mention the tiny fact that you killed the love of my life.'

The complete lack of emotion in Norbert's tone was more frightening than if he'd ranted and raged. The Admiral watched helplessly as he lifted the gun and pointed it towards the hapless boy.

'It wasn't him it was me.' Angela's voice was clear and her father's hand wavered. He frowned and turned towards her. 'What?'

'It was me. I killed my mother.' Angela's voice was defiant and for the first time, Norbert showed some emotion. 'How could you?' he hissed, 'After I'd waited all this time.' He stared disbelievingly at his daughter, then suddenly whispered harshly, 'Why? I saved you five years ago when Michael started prying, I told you that when I came to Dartmouth. I was finally going to take care of you both.'

Angela laughed harshly, 'Oh I'm sure you'd have taken care of us, along with all the money Michael left.'

'I've waited years for what was rightfully mine,' Norbert ground out angrily, 'I am your father, I *deserve* that money.'

'She didn't want you,' Angela spat viciously, 'She made that crystal clear *three* times. She married Barney Bennett – remember? Was his death just a convenient accident?'

The Admiral took a deep breath, wondering if Norbert was going to admit to killing Birdie's third husband, but Angela hadn't finished. She shook her head and continued maliciously, 'You left it far too late to play happy families *daddy*. I loathed my mother and everything she stood for. The lying trollop would open her legs for anyone – well anyone but *you* obviously,' she chuckled maliciously. 'Once was obviously enough...'

The bitter ridicule in her voice finally destroyed her father's fantasy, and with an enraged cry, Norbert Tennant stepped forward and raised his gun, intending to put an end to the daughter he'd never been allowed to acknowledge.

All of a sudden everything happened at once.

The Admiral was about to throw himself at Norbert's feet in a rugby tackle worthy of the Six Nations when fifty pounds of dog streaked out of the darkness and leapt. The gun went off wide, missing its target completely, as Norbert fell backwards, pinned down by an enthusiastic Pickles who promptly sat down on the murderer's chest and wagged his tail. Following him out of the shadows, yelling a battle cry she'd heard on a repeat of *Braveheart* earlier in the week, Mabel came sprinting over, brandishing Jimmy's rounder's bat which she promptly used to bash the prostrate man over the head.

CHAPTER 17

The Admiral climbed to his feet as Angela turned to Joe and hissed, 'Come on, we've got to go.' She took his hand and pulled him, but Joe Wellington just stood rooted to the spot. In the end, Birdie's daughter glanced at him despairingly and took off, the noise of her footfalls quickly swallowed up by the darkness.

The Admiral made no effort to follow her. He'd done his bit, and it was now up to the police to apprehend Marcus Tennant's murderer if they were so inclined. Hurriedly, he went over to Mabel, still bending threateningly over Norbert with her bat in the air, and after gently pulling her away, he checked for a pulse, then uncoiling the rope from his waist, he used it to truss the bastard up like a chicken.

Before he had a chance to go and check on Jimmy, the small man hobbled into the light propped up by Emily who was scolding him mercilessly, in between crying and kissing his cheek. The four elderly sleuths stood and stared wordlessly at each other as Pickles ran backwards and forwards excitedly between them.

'We've called the police,' Mabel offered eventually.

'They should be here in the next half an hour or so,' added Emily.

The Admiral nodded wearily, then frowned. 'How did you get into the castle?' he asked Mabel curiously.

'Just back there,' responded Emily pointing vaguely behind her. 'The wall's collapsed so badly, you can just step over it. Isn't that how you and Jimmy got in?'

Laughing weakly, the Admiral sank to the ground and put his arm around Pickles as the Spaniel attempted to climb onto his lap. A couple of seconds later Jimmy followed suit, then Mabel and Emily until they were sitting in a circle with the two torches on the floor between them pushing back the encroaching darkness.

'Come on Joe,' the Admiral called to the young man who still stood like a statue in the shadows. 'Come and have a sit down over here.'

Wordlessly, Joe came over and sat down and for a few seconds all was silent apart from the slight snores issuing from the mouth of their sleeping murderer.

'So, did you take matters into your own hands and kill Birdie Bennett Joe? Was it like Norbert said?'

The young man shook his head violently. 'I never wanted to hurt her, I only wanted to find out the truth.'

'But you told Angela who you really were.' The tone of the Admiral's voice made it plain that he wasn't asking a question.

Joe hung his head, then looked unhappily over at the Admiral and Jimmy. 'I...I... went to see Birdie when you were in the Isle of Wight. When I got to her house, she was out – only Angela was there. I... I think I was so wound up that I admitted who I was to Angela and confronted her about my father's death.

'At first Angela said she didn't know what I was talking about, that my father's death had been an accident.' He paused and shook his head. 'I called her a liar and went to leave, but she called me back.'

'What happened then?' the Admiral asked sternly when it looked as though Michael's son had said all he was going to.

Joe remained silent, eventually wiping his hand across his face and sniffing. 'She said I was right; Birdie *had* killed my dad. When I asked her why, she broke down and admitted pushing Marcus overboard without his life jacket. According to Angela, she'd just found out that he wasn't her real father, that he... he didn't like women.

'When they unexpectedly had to pull out of the race during Cowes week, she decided to confront him, but she said he refused to discuss it, saying it was neither the time nor the place. Angela told me she was so distraught, she just flipped. She pushed him hard, and he went over.

'As you know, my father was onboard the yacht that day, but he didn't see exactly what happened. It was only later he... he... began asking questions.

'On the day of my dad's death, when they came to this castle for a visit, Birdie went back to the car early. Apparently, my father took the opportunity to ask Angela what had really happened that day on her father's yacht. It seems she insisted the official story was correct and they had an argument when he accused her of refusing to tell him the truth. In the end she stormed off to wait in the car with her mother.

'Evidently, she was in floods of tears when she climbed into the car, so of course Birdie insisted on knowing what had happened. According to Angela, her mother was absolutely furious and went off to confront my dad. Half an hour later he was dead.'

'And Angela suddenly took it into her head to tell you all this?' interrupted Jimmy, disbelief obvious in his voice. 'Did she say why exactly?'

Joe shrugged and sniffed again. 'She said she felt guilty about what happened to my father. She... she...' his voice turned defensive, 'She told me she'd fallen in love with me and wanted us to have a fresh start without any lies on either side.'

'Well to be fair, the lies are pretty big whoppers on her bloody side,' commented the Admiral drily. 'Did Angela actually *tell* you she believed her mother pushed your old man off this battlement here?'

Joe nodded. 'She said they never spoke of it. I think she hated Birdie more because they never actually talked. In Angela's eyes, her mother was a lying trollop – you heard what she said.' He paused and sniffed again, shaking his head. 'If they'd actually spoken to each other, maybe they would have realized that it was Norbert who killed him. Or maybe Birdie already knew that.' He threw his hands up in defeat. There was silence for a while then Joe whispered, 'I didn't know my father was gay.'

'Well given the circumstances, I think we can safely say he batted for both sides,' the Admiral said unsympathetically. 'So, Joe, how did you and Angela end up in Berry Pomeroy Castle with her mother?'

Joe continued staring at the ground and for a few seconds it looked as though he wasn't going to say anything else, then he sighed and finally spoke. 'Angela asked me not to go to the police with what she'd told me. She said we could start a new life away from all of this crap. We could be anyone we wanted to be.' He laughed harshly before continuing, 'I think she thought I was in love with her too. Maybe I was – a little.' He looked up. 'She might be a class A bitch, but deep inside I think she's vulnerable. I honestly do believe she acted on impulse when she pushed Marcus overboard. She was hurting – and still is.'

'Pretty bloody extreme way of showing someone you're a bit miffed with them,' the Admiral responded with raised eyebrows, 'And don't forget your father paid the ultimate price for her so called impulse too.'

'I know that,' Joe responded angrily, 'That's why I came here. I wanted to speak to Birdie myself. Angela had told me her mother killed my dad, but I wanted to ask her *why* she'd killed him. Was it because she was protecting her daughter?' He sighed again, then added, 'I thought maybe I could live with that.'

'So how did you persuade her to come here?' Jimmy asked, waving his hand into the surrounding darkness, 'And where the bloody hell was Birdie when you and Angela were busy playing my lie's bigger than yours?'

'You heard what Norbert said,' Joe responded with a shrug, 'She was at his house telling him about her date with me.'

'That still doesn't explain how you got her to meet with you at a bloody ruined castle,' muttered the Admiral shaking his head.

'I can be very persuasive,' Joe responded, hanging his head in what looked like shame. 'And don't forget she thought she was meeting a man she'd been speaking to online.'

'I can't believe she came here on a date,' murmured Emily aghast. 'It's only weeks since her husband died.'

'Since when has that stopped her?' asked Jimmy drily.

'And she didn't think it was damn strange that some bloke she'd never met suggested meeting in a pile of bollocking ruins?' The Admiral's voice was scathing. 'Who the hell did she think you were – Tarzan?'

Joe shook his head, 'It wasn't like that,' he protested. 'I admit, I didn't tell her who I was, but I've already told you I didn't intend to hurt her. I just wanted to get to the truth.'

'Did Angela know you were secretly wooing her mother?' asked Mabel with a frown, 'You certainly didn't mention it to us when you came for our help.'

'And I ask again,' the Admiral interrupted in exasperation. 'How the bloody hell did you convince Birdie Bennett to go on a date with a complete stranger here of all places?'

'We didn't meet here, we met at the Castle Café. It's actually got a pretty good reputation with the gastro crowd – they've got a French chef apparently - so it wasn't that difficult. We agreed to meet at five o'clock.'

'What was it like?' Emily interjected with interest, 'I've heard very good things. We're thinking of taking a party there from the WI.'

'It was really good,' commented Joe, 'The crab bisque was to die for.'

'But not bloody literally,' interrupted the Admiral, 'And don't change the subject. You can't tell me Birdie wasn't a tad concerned when her date turned out to be someone still wet behind the ears.'

'When she arrived, Angela was with her,' Joe said, his voice clearly showing his irritation at the Admiral's description of him.

'So she wasn't completely convinced you were on the up and up,' Jimmy added sharply, 'Not quite as trusting as us, obviously.'

'So, what happened then?' Emily asked breathlessly – this was becoming more and more like an episode of Hollyoaks every minute.

Joe sat silently for a couple of seconds, and when he continued, his voice sounded weary and wretched. 'I thought Angela was going to give me away, but she didn't tell her mother who I really was. I don't know how she found out about our assignation, but privately she made sure I understood she'd known all along it was me her mother was meeting. I think she'd convinced Birdie to bring her along as support – you know, safety in numbers. What a bloody joke.

'It was Angela who suggested we have a little walk inside the castle. She said there was just enough time before it was due to close.

'By the time we'd eaten, Birdie had made it pretty clear that she wasn't interested in a toy boy. I could tell she just wanted to leave, but Angela persuaded her to stay a little longer.' He laughed mirthlessly. 'I think Birdie actually thought I'd be suitable for her daughter.'

'Well, it's bloody obvious she agreed to have a look round, but how did you get her to stay past closing time?' asked the Admiral scathingly.

Joe closed his eyes and shook his head. 'Angela pushed her down those steps,' he whispered.

'Didn't anyone check the place was empty before they locked up?' the Admiral barked incredulously. 'How the bloody hell did they miss the body?'

'And by my reckoning she'd only been dead a few minutes when we found her,' interrupted Jimmy before Joe could answer, 'Yet you say Angela pushed her over a couple of hours before we got here.'

'What a load of bloody Horlicks,' the Admiral muttered shaking his head, 'I think you better tell us the rest of it before the plod get here.'

Joe buried his head in his hands, and they could see he was shaking. When he finally looked up, tears were cascading down his face.

'I didn't want to hurt her,' he whispered again brokenly. 'I just wanted to find out if she'd killed my father. We were standing in St. Margaret's Tower when I finally plucked up the nerve to admit who I was. But when I asked her if she'd pushed my dad off the battlement, she looked completely stricken. She reached out to me and whispered how sorry she was, that everything had been her fault...'

'But she didn't *actually* admit to killing him,' Jimmy interrupted. Joe frowned, 'Well no, but... well... I assumed...'

'Well, you know what they say about assumption,' the Admiral commented sharply, 'It's the mother of all cock ups – and that certainly holds true in this sorry dit.' He sighed, 'So what happened next?'

'I... I... don't really know exactly what happened next. I know that out of the blue Angela started yelling at Birdie. I couldn't tell what she was saying but she'd completely lost the plot. I couldn't help thinking that's how it must have been when she'd argued with Marcus. Then all of a sudden, she stepped forward and shoved her mother – hard.

'One second Birdie cried out as she fell, and the next there was… silence.' Joe paused to wipe away the tears. 'I just ran,' he murmured. 'I didn't wait to see if she was dead, I… just had to get away.

'Angela came after me and grabbed hold of my arm. She said we needed to look normal to avoid raising any suspicion. Somehow, we got out of the castle just as they were closing. Angela told the caretaker that Birdie had already left, and as we'd been the last to go in, I assume they thought there was no-one else still inside. I wanted to get as far away as possible, but Angela said we had to go back to check she was dead.' He swallowed convulsively and squeezed his eyes shut. 'Once we were sure everyone had gone, we came back in…'

'Just *stepped* over the bloody wall I assume,' the Admiral commented sarcastically. Joe nodded as the Admiral waved him to continue.

'Birdie was lying where we'd left her. She… she was still alive – just. But she was hardly breathing and was definitely unconscious. I said I was going to call an ambulance and before Angela could stop me, I ran out of the tower, looking for a spot where I could get a signal. I think I was a bit out of control by then.' He stopped and looked over at the four elderly people staring at him wordlessly.

'Angela came after me with a knife. We were arguing – and that's where you came in.' He pointed to the Admiral and finished, 'She probably would have killed me too if her father hadn't chosen that moment to intervene.' He shook his head and muttered, 'A crazy bloody family.'

CHAPTER 18

The police arrived half an hour later complete with industrial torches and tracker dogs. Their old friend Detective Chief Inspector Barratt was first on the scene, and after clasping hands with the Admiral and Jimmy in turn, he looked over at the prone form of Norbert Tennant and said, 'I see you've been busy again gentlemen.'

The Admiral led the way to St. Margaret's tower where Birdie's body still lay broken and silent. Joe Wellington confirmed that Angela had pushed her mother down the stairs deliberately as she'd earlier claimed.

After taking brief statements and instructing all of them to attend Crownhill police station the following morning, DCI Barratt ushered them out of the castle, this time using the front gate. The Admiral was tempted to argue, seeing as it was he and Jimmy who'd actually solved the case, but one look at his wobbly friend, changed his mind. It was time to go home. The police could get off their arses and process this crime scene. They'd fill in the rest of the dots at the station tomorrow.

As they walked away from the gate, the Admiral asked Joe if he was okay to drive. The young man nodded without speaking, clearly overcome. Charles Shackleford squeezed his shoulder, this time with a little more sympathy.

It was fully dark now and they needed torches to find their way towards the car park where Mabel and Emily had left the Admiral's car next to Joe's. Angela's unsurprisingly had gone. Hopefully the police would pick her up before too long.

'Are you going to stay on the Dartmouth Belle tonight Joe?' asked Jimmy as they reached the cars. The young man glanced down at his watch and shrugged. 'It's getting on for midnight,' he murmured, 'I think I'll struggle to get a water taxi, and it wouldn't be fair to drag Ben out.'

'Then you can stay with us dear,' Mabel offered immediately. 'We've all got a big day ahead of us tomorrow so it's important you get a good night's sleep.'

'You're no doubt going to be bloody hoarse by the time you've finished recounting your part in the whole cake and arse party,' the Admiral commented wryly. Joe didn't answer, just nodded at Mabel gratefully before opening his boot to pull out a pair of clean trainers.

The Admiral was about to get into his car when he glanced over and saw the shadowed shape of a rucksack in Joe's trunk, highlighted by the young man's torch as he shone it inside to see what he was doing. Charles Shackleford drew in his breath sharply.

Just poking out of the top of the bag was the corner of a neatly stacked bundle of what looked like fifty-pound notes.

∞∞∞

By the time they reached the Admiralty Joe Wellington had vanished. The Admiral and Mabel waited up until two am but there was no sign of him.

At first light, the Admiral called Ben Shepherd and asked him to check if Joe had returned to the Dartmouth Belle. An hour later, Ben reported that the yacht was empty. All of Joe's belongings had been cleared out.

White faced, the Admiral put down the phone and turned to Mabel. 'He's really gone and done a bunk. Joe Wellington spun us a complete bloody pile of shit and we fell for it, hook, line and sinker.'

Mabel sank onto the sofa and shook her head. 'I can't believe it Charlie. I really liked that young man.'

Hurriedly Charles Shackleford got on the phone to Jimmy and an hour later they were all back on the road to Berry Pomeroy Castle.

When they got there, the whole castle was cordoned off, with police guarding the official entrance, and presumably the unofficial one, and crime officers inside. There were a smattering of curious walkers and a couple of reporters from the local press, but the story hadn't made it to prime-time news yet.

It took the four of them about ten minutes to confirm that Birdie had been alone when Joe met up with her the day before. The waitress at the café remembered them mainly because of the obvious age difference. She said they were inside the restaurant for about three quarters of an hour before going into the Castle grounds. She didn't see them come out. She didn't remember seeing Angela at all.

She did however recall seeing a man resembling Norbert Tennant.

Wearily the four of them sat on the terrace outside the café. The Admiral looked down at his watch. It was only nine a.m., but he felt as though he'd been up for hours. He turned to the waitress and asked if they were serving yet. 'Of course,' she smiled, 'Four coffees?'

'Ooh and can I have one of your French guillotines?' asked Mabel excitedly. The waitress frowned in confusion until the elderly matron added, 'With chocolate and banana please.'

'We'll all have a galette,' Emily interrupted firmly, 'I think we could do with the carbohydrates this morning.'

When the waitress had left, Jimmy shook his head and sighed. 'So, the question is,' he commented after a moment, 'Did Angela Tennant pay Joe Wellington to bump off her mother then turn up later to check he'd done the job properly?'

'And if she did, why did she tell old Norbert she'd done it herself. She had to have known he wouldn't take it well.'

'Maybe that's why she did it - you know, to try and make him do something rash to give her enough time to get away. Or perhaps she really had fallen in love with Joe and just wanted to stop her nutcase of a father from blowing her boyfriend's brains out.'

'Well Joe certainly didn't argue with her version of events, did he?'

'Whatever Angela's reasoning, I think we can safely say Norbert's arrival put a bit of a spanner in the works. She definitely wasn't expecting him to drop in.'

'And come to think of it, Norbert never actually mentioned Angela tagging along on Joe and Birdie's so called date, did he?'

'What I can't understand is why he actually told *us* about Angela's horrible offer.'

'That was no doubt before he decided that the cash was more important than his scruples.'

'I'd say murdering someone is a bit more than abandoning your bollocking scruples...'

The Admiral sighed. 'I can't believe we sat there and took everything the lad said as gospel. Joe Wellington played us from the very moment he walked into the Admiralty.'

'He was a very personable young man,' commented Mabel, 'But what *I* can't understand is *why* she wanted Joe to do it at all. I mean, you know - she'd already done one of her parents in and let's be honest, if she wanted her mother gone, it would have been much simpler all round to get it done herself.'

While the other three were left blinking at Mabel's clinical summing up, the Admiral privately decided he'd make every effort to avoid upsetting her any time soon.

'Perhaps she thought it would give her some kind of hold over Joe,' Jimmy reflected, 'You know, two murderers cozying up together – Devon's answer to Bonny and Clyde...'

There was a silence as they all pondered Jimmy's comment.

'Well, to be fair, I did hear Angela saying that it was, 'too soon,' and, 'she wasn't ready,' over the phone to someone. Perhaps that someone was Joe. She could have been having a few scruples of her own,' Emily offered eventually without much conviction.

'Well, if she was, she got over them pretty damn quickly,' the Admiral grunted, shaking his head.

'Anyway,' said Emily briskly as their coffee and French pancakes arrived, 'Whatever her reasoning, it's not our problem anymore.'

'You're right Emily,' agreed the Admiral, brightening as he tucked into the gooey mess on his plate. 'As soon as we've finished here, we'll go straight to Crownhill Police Station and hand the whole bloody cake and arse party over to them.'

It took them over an hour to get to the police station in Plymouth. The two men were silent on the journey, both wondering the same thing. Was everything Joe had told them the night before complete fabrication? Even Mabel and Emily were uncharacteristically silent in the back of the car.

Once there, they were ushered into DCI Barratt's office and the Detective Chief Inspector listened to the whole story without comment. Once they'd finished, he assured them that everything would be done to locate Joe Wellington as soon as possible.

However, he thought they should be aware that Angela Tennant had already been arrested at Exeter airport. When questioned in the early hours, she had confessed to the murders of both her parents.

'My officers asked if anyone else was involved,' continued DCI Barratt, 'But Miss Tennant insisted that she had acted alone on both occasions.'

'But... but... what about all the lies Joe fed us and the money in the back of his car?' blustered the Admiral. 'And why would he have done a bloody runner if he was completely innocent?'

'You can rest assured it's a question we'll certainly be asking Angela, as well as Joe Wellington himself when we finally catch up with him,' responded DCI Barratt calmly.

'What about Norbert Tennant?' Jimmy asked sombrely.

DCI Barratt grinned openly. 'He's currently recovering in hospital from an unexplained smack on the head. He has however been charged with the murder of Michael Wellington and the attempted murder of you two gentlemen. By the way how's your head Mr. Noon?'

Jimmy touched the back of his skull gingerly. 'I'll live Sir, despite the best efforts of your suspect.'

'I'm sure you're in capable hands,' DCI Barratt commented with a warm smile towards Emily who coloured up and giggled slightly.

'Will you re-open the investigation into Barney Bennett's accident?' asked the Admiral. DCI Barratt nodded and stood up. 'We'll keep you appraised of any new findings.' He smiled again, 'Now, if you'll excuse me, I'll leave you in the capable hands of my officers who will take your individual statements. Once again you have my thanks - gentlemen, ladies.'

Shaking their hands in turn, he headed towards the door and hesitated. Turning back, he said wryly, 'If you happen to come across any more potential killers lurking around in your neighbourhood, it might be a good idea if you consider involving us a little earlier. I'd hate for any counts of attempted murder to be elevated to the real thing.'

EPILOGUE

The police never managed to find Joe Wellington. Somehow the young man had vanished into thin air, and as Angela continued to maintain that she'd acted alone, the police eventually lost interest. As to why she would pay Joe to kill her mother, then take the blame for it herself? Perhaps she really had fallen in love with Michael Wellington's son after all.

Barney Bennett's accident turned out to be just that – a tragic accident. Both the Admiral and Jimmy remained convinced that some kind of skullduggery had been afoot, but as both logical suspects were going to be in prison for a very long time, the Admiral was content to let sleeping dogs lie.

That and the fact that Mabel threatened to ask Tory and Noah if they could take Isaac away on holiday for a whole weekend – just the three of them - if he didn't finally put the lid on Operation *Murderous Marriages*…

After all, they'd been instrumental in apprehending two killers – and that should be enough for any self-respecting pensioner, even if one of them is a retired Admiral.

THE END

The Admiral, Jimmy Mabel and Emily return in A *Murderous Season - Book Three of The Admiral Shackleford Mysteries,* now available from Amazon.

Of course, if you haven't yet got around to reading The Shackleford Diaries series and would like to know just how the Admiral was instrumental in getting his daughter Victory hitched to the most famous actor in the world, not to mention all his other shenanigans, all seven books in the series are available on Amazon.

Continue reading to the end for an exclusive sneak peek of *Claiming Victory, Book One of The Shackleford Diaries...*

AUTHOR'S NOTE

The beautiful yachting haven of Dartmouth in South Devon holds a very special place in my heart – not least because I met my husband there :-)

If you're ever in the area, please take the time out to visit. The Floating Bridge, The Ship Inn, and The Royal Castle Hotel are real and I've spent many a happy lunchtime/evening in each of them.

If you'd like more information about Dartmouth and the surrounding areas, visit the Tourist Information Centre.

https://discoverdartmouth.com

To all you Dartmothians out there, I know I missed off the Steam Railway - it was deliberate and I hope you'll forgive me. It just made things too complicated to include…

The Isle of Wight is another beautiful part of the United Kingdom. Just off the south coast of England, it's extremely popular with the yachting crowd and families.

If you'd like more information, you can visit:

https://www.visitisleofwight.co.uk/

And lastly Berry Pomeroy Castle is also a real place and well worth a visit. Both romantic and spooky in turn, my kids did the whole visiting at midnight thing when they were younger – but they only did it once…!

For more information visit:

www.english-heritage.org.uk/visit/places/berry-pomeroy-castle

The Castle Café also exists next to the Castle and I can vouch for the galettes – they really are delicious.

For more information visit:

https://mononclejean.com/who-is-mon-oncle-jean-2

KEEPING IN TOUCH

Thank you so much for reading *A Murderous Marriage* I really hope you enjoyed it.
For any of you who'd like to connect, I'd really love to hear from you. Feel free to contact me via my facebook page: https://www.facebook.com/beverleywattsromanticcomedyauthor or my website: http://www.beverleywatts.com.
If you'd like me to let you know as soon as my next book is available, sign up to my newsletter by copying and pasting the link below and I'll keep you updated about all my latest releases.
https://motivated-teacher-3299.ck.page/143a008c18

Thanks a million for taking the time to read this story. As I mentioned earlier, if you've not yet had your fill of the Admiral's meddling , you might be interested to read the next instalment of *The Admiral Shackleford Mysteries.* Book Three*: A Murderous Season* is available on Amazon.

You might also be interested to learn that the Admiral's Great, Great, Great, Great Grandfather appears in my latest series of lighthearted Regency Romances entitled The Shackleford Sisters.

Book One: *Grace*, Book Two: *Temperance*, Book Three: *Faith* , Book Four: *Hope*, Book Five: *Patience*, Book Six: *Charity*, Book Seven: *Chastity*, Book Eight: *Prudence* and Book Nine: *Anthony* are currently available on Amazon.

And lastly... if you haven't read them yet but think you'd like to give The Shackleford Diaries a go, turn the page for an exclusive sneak peek of *Claiming Victory*, Book One....

CLAIMING VICTORY

Chapter One

Retired Admiral, Charles Shackleford, entered the dimly lit interior of his favourite watering hole. Once inside, he waited a second for his eyes to adjust, and glanced around to check that his ageing Springer spaniel was already seated beside his stool at the bar. Pickles had disappeared into the undergrowth half a mile back, as they walked along the wooded trail high above the picturesque River Dart. The scent of some poor unfortunate rabbit had caught his still youthful nose. The Admiral was not unduly worried; this was a regular occurrence, and Pickles knew his way to the Ship Inn better than his master.

Satisfied that all was as it should be for a Friday lunchtime, Admiral Shackleford waved to the other regulars, and made his way to his customary seat at the bar where his long standing, and long suffering friend, Jimmy Noon, was already halfway down his first pint.

'You're a bit late today Sir,' observed Jimmy, after saluting his former commanding officer smartly.

Charles Shackleford grunted as he heaved his ample bottom onto the bar stool. 'Got bloody waylaid by that bossy daughter of mine.' He sighed dramatically before taking a long draft of his pint of real ale, which was ready and waiting for him. 'Damn bee in her bonnet since she found out about my relationship with Mabel Pomfrey. Of course, I told her to mind her own bloody business, but it has to be said that the cat's out of the bag, and no mistake.'

He stared gloomily down into his pint. 'She said it cast aspersions on her poor mother's memory. But what she doesn't understand Jimmy, is that I'm still a man in my prime. I've got needs. I mean look at me – why can't she see that I'm still a fine figure of a man, and any woman would be more than happy to shack up with me.'

Abruptly, the Admiral turned towards his friend so the light shone directly onto his face and leaned forward. 'Come on then man, tell me you agree.'

Jimmy took a deep breath as he dubiously regarded the watery eyes, thread veined cheeks, and larger than average nose no more than six inches in front of him

However, before he could come up with a suitably acceptable reply that wouldn't result in him standing to attention for the next four hours in front of the Admiral's dishwasher, the Admiral turned away, either indicating it was purely a rhetorical question, or he genuinely couldn't comprehend that anyone could possibly regard him as less than a prime catch.

Jimmy sighed with relief. He really hadn't got time this afternoon to do dishwasher duty as he'd agreed to take his wife shopping. Although to be fair, a four hour stint in front of an electrical appliance at the Admiral's house, with Tory sneaking him tea and biscuits, was actually preferable to four hours trailing after his wife in Marks and Spencer's. He didn't think his wife would see it that way though. Emily Noon had enough trouble understanding her husband's tolerance towards 'that dinosaur's' eccentricities as it was.

Of course, Emily wasn't aware that only the quick thinking of the dinosaur in question had, early on in their naval career, saved her husband from a potentially horrible fate involving a Thai prostitute who'd actually turned out to be a man...

As far as Jimmy was concerned, Admiral Shackleford was his Commanding Officer, and always would be, and if that involved such idiosyncrasies as presenting himself in front of a dishwasher with headphones on, saluting and saying, 'Dishwasher manned and ready sir.' Then four hours later, saluting again while saying, 'Dishwasher secured,' so be it.

It was a small price to pay... He leaned towards his morose friend and patted him on the back, showing a little manly support (acceptable, even from subordinates), while murmuring, 'Don't worry about it too much Sir. Tory's a sensible girl. She'll come round eventually – you know she wants you to be happy.' The Admiral's only response was an inelegant snort, so Jimmy ceased his patting, and went back to his pint.

Both men gazed into their drinks for a few minutes, as if all the answers would be found in the amber depths.

'What she needs is a man.' Jimmy's abrupt observation drew another rude snort, this one even louder.

'Who do you suggest? She's not interested in anyone. Says there's no one in Dartmouth she'd give house room to, and believe me I've tried. When she's not giving me grief, she spends all her time in that bloody gallery with all those airy fairy types. Can't imagine any one of them climbing her rigging. Not one set of balls between 'em.' Jimmy chuckled at the Admiral's description of Tory's testosterone challenged male friends.

'She's not ugly though,' Charles Shackleford mused, still staring into his drink. 'She might have an arse the size of an aircraft carrier, but she's got her mother's top half which balances it out nicely.'

'Aye, she's built a bit broad across the beam,' Jimmy agreed nodding his head.

'And then there's this bloody film crew. I haven't told her yet.' Jimmy frowned at the abrupt change of subject, and shot a puzzled glance over to the Admiral.

'Film crew? What film crew?'

Charles Shackleford looked back irritably. 'Come on Jimmy, get a grip. I'm talking about that group of nancies coming to film at the house next month. I must have mentioned it.'

Jimmy simply shook his head in bewilderment.

Frowning at his friend's obtuseness, the Admiral went on, 'You know, what's that bloody film they're making at the moment – big blockbuster everyone's talking about?'

'What, you mean The Bridegroom?'

'That's the one. Seems like they were looking for a large house overlooking the River Dart. Think they were hoping for Greenway, you know, Agatha Christie's place, but then they spied "the Admiralty" and said it was spot on. Paying me a packet they are. Coming next week.'

Jimmy stared at his former commanding officer with something approaching pity. 'And you've arranged all this without telling Tory?'

'None of her bloody business,' the Admiral blustered, banging his now empty pint glass on the bar, and waving at the barmaid for a refill. 'She's out most of the time anyway.'

Jimmy shook his head in disbelief. 'When are you going to tell her?'

'Was going to do it this morning, but then this business with Mabel came up so I scarpered. Last I saw she was taking that bloody little mongrel of hers out for a walk. Hoping she'll walk off her temper.' His tone indicated he considered there was more likelihood of hell freezing over.

'Is Noah Westbrook coming?' said Jimmy, suddenly sensing a bit of gossip he could pass on to Emily.

'Noah who?' was the Admiral's bewildered response.

'Noah Westbrook. Come on Sir, you must know him. He's the most famous actor in the world. Women go completely gaga over him. If nothing else, that should make Tory happy.'

The Admiral stared at him thoughtfully. 'What's he look like, this Noah West... chappy?'

The barmaid, who had been unashamedly listening to the whole conversation, couldn't contain herself any longer and, thrusting a glossy magazine under the Admiral's nose, said breathlessly, 'Like this. He looks like this.'

The full colour photograph was that of a naked man lounging on a sofa, with only a towel protecting his modesty, together with the caption "Noah Westbrook, officially voted the sexiest man on the planet."

Admiral Charles Shackleford stared pensively down at the picture in front of him. 'So this Noah chap – he's in this film is he?'

'He's got the lead role.' The bar maid actually twittered causing the Admiral to look up in irritation – bloody woman must be fifty if she's a day. Shooting her a withering look, he went back to the magazine, and read the beginning of the article inside.

"Noah Westbrook is to be filming in the South West of England over the next month, causing a sudden flurry of bookings to hotels and guest houses in the South Devon area."

The Admiral continued to stare at the photo, the germination of an idea tiptoeing around the edges of his brain. Glancing up, he discovered he was the subject of scrutiny from not just the barmaid, but now the whole pub was waiting with baited breath to hear what he was going to say next.

The Admiral's eyes narrowed as the beginnings of a plan slowly began taking shape, but he needed to keep it under wraps. Looking around at his rapt audience, he feigned nonchalance. 'Don't think Noah Westbrook was mentioned at all in the correspondence. Think he must be filming somewhere else.'

Then, without saying anything further, he downed the rest of his drink, and climbed laboriously off his stool.

'Coming Jimmy, Pickles?' His tone was deceptively casual which fooled Jimmy not at all, and, sensing something momentous afoot, the smaller man swiftly finished his pint. In his haste to follow the Admiral out of the door, he only narrowly avoided falling over Pickles who, completely unappreciative of the need for urgency, was sitting in the middle of the floor, scratching unconcernedly behind his ear.

Once outside, the Admiral didn't bother waiting for his dog, secure in the knowledge that someone would let the elderly spaniel out before he got too far down the road. Instead, he took hold of Jimmy's arm, and dragged him out of earshot – just in case anyone was listening.

In complete contrast to his mood on arrival, Charles Shackleford was now grinning from ear to ear. 'That's it. I've finally got a plan,' he hissed to his bewildered friend. 'I'm going to get her married off.'

'Who to?' asked Jimmy confused.

'Don't be so bloody slow Jimmy. To him of course. The actor chappy, Noah Westbrook. According to that magazine, women everywhere fall over themselves for him. Even Victory won't be able to resist him.'

Jimmy opened his mouth but nothing came out. He stared in complete disbelief as the Admiral went on. 'Then she'll move out, and Mabel can move in. Simple.'

Pickles came ambling up as Jimmy finally found his voice. 'So, let me get this straight Sir. Your plan is to somehow get Noah Westbrook, the most famous actor on the entire planet to fall in love with your daughter Victory, who we both love dearly, but - and please don't take offence Sir - who you yourself admit is built generously across the aft, and whose face is unlikely to launch the Dartmouth ferry, let alone a thousand ships.'

The Admiral frowned. 'Well admittedly, I've not worked out the finer details, but that's about the sum of it. What do you think…?'

Claiming Victory is available from Amazon

Turn the page for a full list of all my books available on Amazon.

ALSO AVAILABLE BY BEVERLEY WATTS ON AMAZON

The Shackleford Diaries:
Book 1 - Claiming Victory
Book 2 - Sweet Victory
Book 3 - All For Victory
Book 4 - Chasing Victory
Book 5 - Lasting Victory
Book 6 - A Shackleford Victory
Book 7 - Final Victory

The Admiral Shackleford Mysteries
Book 1 - A Murderous Valentine
Book 2 - A Murderous Marriage
Book 3 - A Murderous Season

The Shackleford Sisters
Book 1 - Grace
Book 2 - Temperance
Book 3 - Faith
Book 4 - Hope
Book 5 - Patience

Book 6 - Charity
Book 7 - Chastity
Book 8 - Prudence
Book 9 - Anthony

The Shackleford Legacies
Book 1 - Jennifer
Book 2 - Mercedes
Book 3 - Roseanna
Book 4 - Henrietta will be released on 20th December 2025

Shackleford and Daughters
Book 1 - Alexandra will be released on 12th June 2025

Standalone Titles
An Officer and a Gentleman Wanted

ABOUT THE AUTHOR

Beverley Watts

Beverley spent 8 years teaching English as a Foreign Language to International Military Students in Britannia Royal Naval College, the Royal Navy's premier officer training establishment in the UK. She says that in the whole 8 years there was never a dull moment and many of her wonderful experiences at the College were not only memorable but were most definitely 'the stuff of fiction.' Her debut novel An Officer And A Gentleman Wanted is very loosely based on her adventures at the College.

Beverley particularly enjoys writing books that make people laugh and currently she has three series of Romantic Comedies, both contemporary and historical, as well as a humorous cosy mystery series under her belt.

She lives with her husband in an apartment overlooking the sea on the beautiful English Riviera. Between them they have 3 adult children and two gorgeous grandchildren plus 3 Romanian rescue dogs of indeterminate breed called Florence, Trixie, and Lizzie. Until recently, they also had an adorable 'Chichon" named Dotty who was the inspiration for Dotty in The Shackleford Diaries.

You can find out more about Beverley's books at www.beverley-watts.com

Printed in Dunstable, United Kingdom